Altar Boys Anonymous

A Collection of Short Stories

by

D. E. Macías, Ph.D.

Altar Boys Anonymous
A Collection of Short Stories

by

D. E. Macías, Ph.D.

Published By
Positive Imaging, LLC
https://positive-imaging.com
bill@positive-imaging.com

ISBN: 9781951776916

Table of Contents

Author's Notes and Preface

to

Altar Boys Anonymous

Disclaimers (of a sort):

These short stories are works of fiction, so to speak. Some of the characters were actual living beings, but I have changed their names and have changed the circumstances surrounding them. Their names and the places associated with them do not represent any living or deceased person accurately. They have been fictionalized in much the same way someone copies a Picasso.

Most of the characters are people I have known at some level and to some degree, but I must emphasize that in the story, these are fictional characters based loosely on people I have actually known. Some characters are totally fictitious, including narrators. Time wise, the relevant events primarily take place within a 50 year period, 1953 to 2003.

Facts are actually alternate facts associated with the characters, and are included for dramatic embellishment. Accuracy of some facts may sometimes be subjective and not meant to be absolute. Artistic freedom is to be understood and accepted by the reader.

Acknowledgments

I wish to thank the members of The Writers' Roundtable of the Northeast Senior Center in San Antonio, Texas for their input and support. Also I would like to acknowledge the professional assistance of A. William Benitez @ Positive Imaging, LLC Publishing.

Introduction

These stories are loosely organized with little chronological order. Nevertheless, as a trained psychologist, I have attempted to sequence characters' stages of development.

Back in the 50s and 60s, many Mexican American kids grew up poor, in a poor area of town, on the other side of the tracks, you might say. They were not aware of the concept of poverty, nor of social classifications. Some ended up taking a wrong turn; then regretting it later. Fortunately for Ricky, he had loving parents and caring teachers. He was not cognizant of this at the time. But he would become mindful of that in later years.

Ricky is a little boy in elementary school who still has a lot to learn about life and how to relate to the people in his life. His innocence and youth should not be excuses for his thoughts and behaviors. Because, like most children, his mental and behavioral expressions will change over time with maturity. (Or at least, that's the way it's supposed to be.)

Sister San Juan

"More things are wrought by prayer

Than this world dreams of."

-- Tennyson (1809-1892) Morte d'Arthur

Eleven-year-old Ricky asked "Why do nuns have men's names, mom?"

"I'm not sure, but I think their names are given to them by the Order."

"Well, is it because they ran out of women's names?"

"No. Nuns take the names of saints, and most saints are men."

"Oh! I see! So there's a good chance a nun could take my name ... Sister Ricky"

"You're not a saint. You're just an altar boy."

During the week, Ricky would serve at Mass every morning before going to school, which was less than a block away.

In those days, primary or elementary school went up to the 8th grade, and the student would graduate to secondary, which was high school, grades 9 through 12. Middle school would emerge some years later. The primary school Ricky attended was a Catholic (parochial) school, and was located just a few blocks from the family's home. The school building was erected on a slope and consisted of only two levels and had no air conditioning back then. In hot weather, large windows were left open during the day, and the warm air from outside could be felt flowing through the classrooms and hallways. There were also squeaky ceiling fans, which often did not function. Nevertheless, the school had a pleasant, comfortable, "home-like" atmosphere.

Most of the teachers at the elementary level were nuns of the Order of St. Joseph. They wore heavy black garments (habits) with a stiff white, cardboard-like, starched guimpe (bib or wimple), and coif headdresses, a crucifix hanging from the neck to the chest. The sisters always wore a long black rosary around their waist. They came from all over the U.S., but no foreigners. Then there was Sister San Juan.

Born in the U.S., Sister San Juan somehow seemed foreign. She was short, had very dark brown skin, and she spoke perfect English, but also perfect Spanish. And she was old. She was the oldest sister at the school. The students thought that she might be around 100 years old. But in truth, she was in her 60s. And, by all standards, she could be described as just plain 'mean'. All the students both feared and hated her...nay, they despised her. To the parents of the students, she was just a strict and a forceful disciplinarian. Parents liked Sister San Juan.

Ricky Martinez did not like Sister San Juan. To him, she was a witch...a mean old lady whom even God was afraid of. She often made Ricky stand in the back of the room for being "disruptive" and for being downright "a pain in the neck" (her words). In addition, she would hit him with a ruler if he talked out of turn. It was serious when she went for the yardstick. That meant that he would get an even harsher punishment. When she wasn't hitting him or making him stand in the back of the room, she would have him write 100 times on the board "I am a disobedient little boy who needs to be disciplined", or keep him after school to do her dirty, clean-up work. No... Ricky and Sister San Juan did not have a good relationship. She was master, and he was slave.

He thought *Maybe she wouldn't be so mean if she didn't have to wear that heavy old black costume.* He shuddered as he imagined what she might look like out of her costume. *Maybe she's mean because she hates little boys and didn't want to teach at this poor, little school in the barrio. Maybe her mother was mean to her, and that's why she is mean to all kids. Maybe, just maybe, she's even angry at God for making her a nun when she really wanted to meet a rich man and get married and have a lot of children, mostly girls. Yeah, that makes more sense.*

When Ricky finally graduated 8th grade, it was none too soon. He would no longer have to put up with Sister San Juan. He could now go to high school elsewhere, far enough away from Sister and her yardstick, and he would be free and happy and no longer afraid of being punished for really stupid things. At the graduation ceremony, Sister San Juan came up to Ricky and his parents and said "Now Ricky, you be a good boy in high school and study hard...really hard. And then maybe, who knows, maybe college?"

"I will, Sister. And, I'm going to miss you, Sister!" he said with a grin.

"Oh, no. I don't think you will miss me at all, Ricardo (using his birth name)." She glanced at his parents and smiled knowingly. "But you will remember me. And someday... maybe someday you will miss me, and you will be glad that you had me as a teacher and, yes, even glad that I was so 'mean' to you. Let's just say I was strict with you!"

Ricky thought to himself *No way, Nun. No way!* Sister San Juan and his parents exchanged a few niceties, and then it was over. The family left the school assembly room, and Ricky, in his mind, if not his heart, said good-bye to that poor little school and to mean, old Sister San Juan.

After elementary school, high school felt like being released from jail. The high school, named after a famous Irish Bishop, was primarily Hispanic and African American, and was also a parochial school, with secular teachers and a few nuns. But the nuns were much nicer and not very strict. Ricky was able to manipulate a few of them while he enjoyed being a typical, rowdy, high school teenager. He felt free to "spread his wings" and have a great time while in high school.

He studied ... sometimes. But when he slacked in the academic area, he felt guilty. He hated feeling guilty for going out with his friends instead of studying for an upcoming exam. He felt guilty for putting fun before study. Where was this guilt coming from? His friends did not feel this way. He thought of Sister San Juan's advice "Study hard ... really hard."

One day, he said out loud "Damn it! It's her fault I'm feeling guilty for not studying." And so, he began to apply himself, committing to study as best he could.

Four years of high school passed quickly. Ricky ended up being a slightly above average student, earning Bs in almost all of his classes. He thought about why he got mostly Bs, and hardly any As. Then it occurred to him that he would have gotten mostly Cs, if he had not studied as much as he did. Although, deep down he knew that he could have studied a lot more and a lot harder than he did. It seemed that whenever he did get down to studying, it was because he thought of Sister San Juan.

Now, because his grades were not that bad, he could apply to college, which he had not thought about since

Sister San Juan's comment. College! Yes, he would be the first in his family to go to college...maybe even a University. Wow!

He applied to several colleges and universities. And to his and his parents' surprise, he was accepted at several. He chose one school not far from his hometown and his family, one which had a good program in the subjects and area he was interested in.

Life was good. Life was going to be peachy! But first, he would work all summer and save his money so that he could spare his parents some of the college expense. He was fortunate enough to get a job with a landscaping company. He worked hard and saved a good deal of money. With the extra money, he was able to put a down payment on an older model car.

At the end of the summer, when his work came to an end, he went to pick up his last paycheck. His boss handed him the check and said "Ricky, you have been one of the best summer workers I've hired in the 20 years I've been doing this kind of work. I don't know where you got your work ethic, but you sure have a lot of self-discipline and determination. I wish you the best in college. And if you ever want to come back and work for me, like during the summer, you will always have a job here. Good luck to you, young man."

Ricky thanked him, shook his boss's hand in a manly way, and left. His heart was pounding. He was so proud of himself. He felt good. His boss had told him that he had self-discipline and determination. He smiled and thought *Take that, Sister San Juan! I'm not that little snot-nose kid who you can push around anymore. You'll see. I won't let you get me down ever again. Those days are history, Baby.*

College was difficult. It was very demanding, structured, organized, and big. Courses were tough and stressful. So many students! So many really smart students!

They were so smart that they did not have to study hard, and they still made good grades. And so many distractions! The late-night parties. The girls. The booze. The drugs. The fun...and yes, the sex. It was overwhelming. A far cry from the little elementary school in the barrio.

But once again, the spirit of Sister San Juan surfaced from within him. He told himself "I must study, and I must study hard. I have to discipline myself because there is no one here to do it for me. I can't let all the distractions take me away from my goal -- which is to graduate from college with really good grades so that mom and dad and.... well, mom and dad would be proud of me. And I can be proud of myself."

And so, he buckled down to study, to learn. He took advantage of all the opportunities that college had to offer. He was a man now. He did not need someone with a ruler or a yardstick standing over him. He could do this. He could do this himself. He mused *"I am not a disobedient boy. I am a man who is obedient to his own mind, his own soul, and his own heart."*

Four years at College flew by. Ricky had applied to Graduate School at another University, far from home, and had been accepted into its Physics program. On the day of college graduation, a Saturday, his mother cried, which meant she too was proud of him. His dad bragged, which did not mean much to Ricky. He was just glad that it was over; and he was looking forward to graduate school.

Mr. Duran would hire him back to do landscaping for the summer, as he had the past four summers. Then Ricky might take a short vacation at the end of August, with Valerie, a girl he met in college, before he headed off for graduate school. Those were his plans. Except that....

Walking with his parents to the car at the end of Commencement, Ricky's mom turned to him. "I hope you don't have plans for next weekend."

"I don't think so", he replied quizzically.

"Well, I hope you don't mind, *hijo* (son), but I need you to take Sister San Juan to San Antonio on Sunday. I told her you would do it."

Ricky stepped back. "What? Mom, I don't want to take Sister Terrorist anywhere ... ever. Besides, she hates me."

"She doesn't hate you. Look, I promised her that you would take her. No one else is available to take her. She officially retires from teaching next Saturday, and she will be spending the rest of her days in sort of nun's retirement center in San Antonio. And you know it's not that far... just down the Interstate."

"But mom, why did you promise her? And what do you mean no one else is available?" Ricky looked at his dad.

"Don't look at me," said his dad. "I'm at the warehouse all weekend."

"Mom..." Ricky pleaded, whining.

"Please, Ricky. She seemed so excited and happy when I told her that you would be happy to drive her. Even though you think she never showed it, she does love you. Please. Do this for me if not for her. Please."

He tightened his lips, and then spoke without moving them "Okay."

He had asked Valerie to go with him, to act as a kind of buffer between him and Sister San Juan. However, she suddenly had other commitments. So, Sunday morning, after a tasty and filling breakfast, Ricky, alone, drove his dad's old station wagon to the residency to pick up Sister San Juan. He borrowed the station wagon because his mom told him that Sister may have some large pieces of luggage to take with her. Ricky had commented "I thought nuns didn't hold on to material things...you know, poverty and all that." His mother ignored him.

As he entered the circle driveway of the nun's residency, he immediately laid eyes on a tiny, frail, old lady in nun's habit.... Sister San Juan. He had not seen her in many years. She was surrounded by suitcases, boxes, and bags, and about a dozen nuns, also in habit. He thought *Oh my God! This will surely put me to the test!*

"Ricky, Ricky. You're right on time. God bless you, my good boy" she smiled.

He had never seen her so happy, nor look so old. All the other nuns were talking and giving their blessings and farewell messages to Sister, and there was much gaiety and joy. They were like family...they were like sisters...real sisters...blood sisters. Much hugging and kissing and tears of joy.

Ricky loaded the items into the station wagon. He said good-bye to the nuns. Sister said good-bye to the nuns; and off they were for the nearly four-hour drive. Sister turned to Ricky and said "Thank you so much, Ricky. I really do appreciate it. But of course, you owe me. And thank your mother again for me. I am so happy today. Do you know I even feel like dancing?"

Hold up there, Sister Ricky thought. *What do you mean 'I owe' you?* He thought this, but did not say it aloud to Sister. Instead, he resigned to say very little during this trip. He thought *It's too late to try to be nice to me, Sister. The damage is done.* So he decided to take a safe and stress-free approach. He would make minimal, harmless conversation with her.

"Dancing, Sister? I can't imagine you dancing."

"I know. You think that all I do is teach and punish children."

The comment was a rhetorical one. It did not deserve a retort. He reminded himself that he would remain safe and agreeable with his words. But... there was nothing to keep him from expressing himself nonverbally.

Once on the highway, he decided *I'll teach this Nazi nun a little something. This little disobedient student is going to teach the teacher a little lesson.* He slowly pressed on the accelerator. The car began to go faster; then faster; then faster. He started weaving between cars to pass them, changing lanes quickly. In a word, he was driving recklessly. Several times he came very close to another car, and then quickly averted an accident.

Sister San Juan grabbed her rosary. Squeezing each bead one at a time, she quietly, lips moving, began to pray the Rosary. Ricky grinned...*Good! I'm scaring her.* After almost an hour of this, he realized that his dad had not filled the gas tank and that the meter was now reading on LOW. A few miles down the highway, he turned off toward a service station to fill up on gas. Sister San Juan sighed and seemed relieved.

After filling the car with gas, Ricky got back into the driver's seat, ready to resume his "adventure."

"Ricky", sister said softly. "I wish you wouldn't drive so recklessly. We have plenty of time. Would you please drive more safely?"

"Oh, did I scare you, sister? Well, I didn't mean to. Are you worried about your safety?"

"No, Ricky. I'm worried about you. I don't want anything bad to happen to you. You're a young man now. I'm an old lady going to a place where I will soon die. I'm not afraid of death. I'm not afraid for my safety."

"But I saw you praying the Rosary."

"I was praying for you, for your safety...always."

"You weren't worried about my safety when you punished me for being a disobedient kid in elementary school" he retorted.

"Oh, I see. That's what this is all about...Ricky, I'm sorry if you thought I was mean to you and the other kids when I had you in school. But to tell you the truth, I was that way with all of you because I loved you all so very much. And I knew that if I were really strict with you, that you would turn out well. I don't know if what I did made you a better person. But I can tell you, now, you are a better person, for whatever reason. I'd like to think I had a small part in that."

He did not respond. He started the car and decided to drive more carefully from here on out. There was silence in the car for a long time. He turned on the radio to break the silence. Sister reached over and turned it off.

"Ricky, when I was a very little girl, an only child, I wanted to become a nun. I knew from a very early age that someday I would be a nun. I knew that God wanted me to be a nun. I had a "calling". My parents were clearly disappointed, because they were hoping I'd marry and give them grandchildren. What parent doesn't want this for and from their children? It makes me sad that I never gave them grandchildren. But that sadness is tempered by the joy and satisfaction I have been given over the past 60 years by being a nun... by being Sister San Juan.

"My parents died when I was in my second year as a nun. I never knew I could experience such sadness. Take care of your parents, Ricky. No matter what your relationship with them, take care of them, because someday they will be gone. I pray for my parents almost every day. I never pray for myself. I never ask God for anything for me. My prayers are prayers of thanks and praise. God knows what I want in my heart and what I need. I don't need to ask for anything. He gives me just what I need and sometimes what I want. He's funny that way."

Ricky listened intently, while at the same time focusing on the highway.

Sister continued. "Soon after my parents died, and they died 3 months apart... my mother first and then daddy...soon after my parents died, I was told by Mother Superior that I would be teaching at a beautiful, up-scale high school in Chicago. She said that the kids came from middle-class families, and that the nuns' living quarters there were first-class. That's what Mother Superior called it "up-scale", "first-class." She told me I was very lucky to be selected to go there. I remember she detected that I was not very pleased with being sent to an "up-scale" place. After a nun gets an assignment outside the convent, she is no longer a nun, but becomes a Catholic Sister. That's a title change most people don't understand. Nuns are rarely seen outside the convent or cloister. Sisters, you see, are involved in communities.

"That night, I prayed, and I thanked God for this opportunity. But then I quietly ended my prayer saying 'Thy will be done, but grant that Thy will be to send me to a place where I can do the most good...to a place with the most need. Amen.'

"The next day, Mother Superior again called me in and said 'Sister, yesterday when I gave you the news about sending you to Chicago, I got the sense that you were not too agreeable to the idea. Now, I usually don't consider whether an assignment is agreeable to the subordinate or not. We sisters took a vow of obedience, so we go where we are sent, and we do what we are told. So, because you may not like where we had decided to send you, I, we, have changed our minds -- as a minor, let's say 'punishment', for your subtle display of pride. For the time being, I'm going to send you to a small, elementary school in a poor area near Houston ... in the hope that you will learn a little humility. I hope you understand why I find it necessary to make this change. It is for your own good.... You may go now.'

"Mother Superior was right. It was for my own good, and it was God's will. I was never so happy in my life. Never so happy...at least not until now. At this moment, I am very happy. Are you happy, Ricky?"

Ricky did not respond for a few minutes. He thought *She has always known that she would be a nun. She has always known what she wanted to do. I don't even know what I'm going to be doing next week. Could it be possible that she really did have my interests at heart? Have I been hating her all these years because she wanted me to grow up to be a better person?* His throat and mouth were dry. But he spoke as best he could.

"I would say I'm pretty happy, Sister. And one more thing, Sister. You married Christ. You honored your parents by becoming a teacher to the children and grandchildren of others, thousands of them. I was one of them." His eyes on the road, he smiled.

"And by the way, Sister, why do nuns, I mean Sisters, have men's names? That's weird!"

"Well, we are of course asked to surrender our birth name and to take the name of a saint. I chose Saint John, San Juan, because that was my daddy's name, John. The Order does not care if the name is male or female."

"And what was your given name at birth? You know, on your birth certificate?"

"Grace."

"Grace. I like that" Ricky said.

They did not speak again until they arrived at the nun's retirement center. It was a beautiful place, secluded and off the main roadway; yet the atmosphere seemed humble. There were more nuns who came out to greet and welcome their new resident. Most of them were very old, but they all appeared happy and content.

Ricky unloaded the bags, boxes, and suitcases, and a middle-aged man who only spoke Spanish carried them into the building. Sister introduced Ricky to the other nuns and them to him. She seemed to know all of them. Family. The nuns offered him a soft drink and asked him to stay for a meal. He politely declined and explained that he wanted to get back home before it got too late.

"Thank you, again, Ricky. You must know how much this has meant to me. I will always pray for you and your family."

"Thanks, Sister. And may you have a good and holy life. Good-bye now."

And with that, as the nuns waved to him, he got into the car and began the long drive home. He could see the nuns still waving at him through the rear-view mirror, while at the same time hugging each other. Alone in the car, with the radio off, he had time to reflect. How blessed he was! How blessed to have parents who cared about him! To have had teachers and professors, and friends who loved him and cared about him! And seeing the nuns say good-bye to Sister that morning; and now the other nuns greet and welcome Sister San Juan, he could only believe that they both loved and cared about each other in such a blessed and holy way.

How great is that? Sister San Juan: Saint or Terrorist? He laughed to himself, and he thought of the words of St. Paul, which he could only paraphrase: *When I was a child I spoke like a child, and I thought like a child. Now that I am a man...* Now that he was a man, Ricky could put away "some" things" of the child. *Sister San Juan is*, he thought, *probably a saint.* He also realized that he would never see her again; that she would soon pass on.

He got back to his parents' home just in time for dinner. His dad arrived at about the same time. At the table, his mother asked "Well, how'd it go?"

"Okay. Actually, it went very well. Sister turned out to be a pretty cool lady."

"Oh, really? I thought you hated her?" his dad posited.

"I don't know that I hated her. I just didn't like her. But that was a long time ago. I've learned a lot since those elementary school days."

"And so now you like that mean, old nun? Scoop me some rice on there, would you, honey?" His dad gestured to the bowl of rice.

Ricky hesitated. "Well ... I guess I was too young to realize that she always was, and is, basically, a very good person."

His mom agreed "Sister San Juan is a really good human being...a good person. In fact, the nuns... all of them... they're all good people."

Ricky concurred "Yeah, they are all good. Save me some of that rice!"

Years later, Ricky and Valerie were happily married and soon had a daughter.

When he learned of Sister San Juan's passing, Ricky, holding their first-born in his arms, bent his head down and kissed the forehead of the infant child they named Grace.

Introduction

There is a special bond within family. It is sometimes positive and sometimes negative. Still, there are ties that tangle and untangle in rhythm. Grandparents are special, because they have history and years of learning. Often times, grandparents love their grandchildren more than they love their own children. And vice versa.

Such was the relationship between Tommy and his grandparents. He felt closer to them because in his early development, he spent most of his 'imprinting' years with them.

To experience loss at an early age is also a unique experience. It is often an existential challenge for children. Tommy would learn about loss, death, at an early age. He would carry those losses with him for the rest of his life. Tommy had two loving *abuelos*.
Let me allow Tommy to share his story!

Grandpa Jēsus

Gratitude is the sign of noble souls.

-- Aesop (6th C. B.C.) *Androcles*

It was an average cold and icy December day in Nebraska. The ground was covered with snow, and a merciless wind blew in from the north. The chain of cars made their way through the narrow drive dividing the two sides of the cemetery like a frozen river; gravestones to the left and to the right of us.

We were there that day to bury Grandpa. Unlike Grandma, he had died quietly in his sleep three days earlier. Many of the town's people were at the cemetery to pay their respects. They all knew and loved this old man they called *Jēsus*, as in Jesus Christ. Family and close friends used the Spanish pronunciation *hey soos*.

After the priest read a few prayers and blessings, members of the immediate family scooped dirt from a bucket and scattered it over the casket. Ashes to ashes, dust to dust, as The Book of Common Prayer says. The cemetery caretaker then attempted to lower the casket into the ground, but the mechanism would not budge. It had frozen, like the ground we stood on. Under these conditions, the caretakers would normally lower the casket manually. But there was only one caretaker that day, and he said he would have to wait a while before the machine would work. The mourners decided to go home and leave the man to handle it later as the temperature warmed. The casket remained exposed above ground as we made our way back to our cars.

Almost everyone was crying, except me. I was sad, but I was having a delayed response to Grandpa's passing. I was thinking about his life; how it all came to a quiet finale on that day. You see, in my mind, he was still alive inside me, even up to seeing the casket suspended above the hole in the ground.

His journey began in Mexico many years ago. He had fallen in love with a fifteen-year old girl. He was nineteen or so and wanted to marry her. But her family said that she was too young. The story goes that he took her aside and told her that he was going to go to America and make a lot of money. He wanted her to go with him. Sometime later, maybe months or a year, to the dismay of both families, Grandpa and his young bride were gone. Disappeared!

They had eloped, were married by a Justice of the Peace, and had headed north to the Mexican-American border. Her family reported her kidnapped. The authorities went looking for the vanished duo. But they were not to be found. They were already riding in a cattle car and headed toward the US-Mexican border crossing to the North.

The year was somewhere between 1915 and 1918. America was involved in the First World War. There was a paucity of male workers in America, so immigration rules were temporarily relaxed to allow foreigners to enter the country from Mexico to work. At the Texas border, Grandpa and Grandma were questioned and interviewed, and their names were recorded on an immigration manifest before being allowed legal entrance.

According to Grandpa, the Texans poured kerosene all over the two of them. The Texans explained "We're doing this because you people might be carrying disease or some other kind of contagious thing." This infuriated Grandpa, so when they were offered temporary housing in Texas, he declined, telling Grandma "I'll be damned if we'll stay in this state. Let's get back on a train and get the hell out of here before they do something worse to us."

They boarded a different train, a passenger car actually. When asked by the authorities how far they were going to go, Grandpa said "Just keep going north, out of this state, and I'll let you know when we want to get off." The security officer did not argue or ask again. It apparently did not matter to the conductor where they got off; just as long as they did not bother anyone.

Five days later, they had made it as far north as Kansas City. But they did not get off, because Grandpa said that the city was too big. A few hours later they were in Nebraska. A fellow passenger, also an immigrant from Mexico, asked Grandpa where he was planning to get off. He told Grandpa that he should go with everyone else all the way to Chicago, the last stop on this train route. Grandpa said Chicago was also too big.

As the train came to a stop in a small remote area of eastern Nebraska, Grandpa said "We'll get off here." And so they did. Grandma was just happy to finally get off the train. She had a bad case of motion sickness. It was a beautiful spring day, and the quaint, little town reminded them of their humble village, the pueblo they left back in Mexico. Grandpa liked the "the smell of the place."

They had little money, but enough to put a down-payment on an old house built in the mid-1800s. Grandpa checked in with the city government to establish residency in the area. He was immediately offered a job at an iron foundry as a moulder. He was also offered a part-time job with the railroad, the AT&SF. Things were moving fast. Life in America was looking better.

Grandpa never learned to speak English fluently. He learned just enough to get by. His receptive skills were much better than his expressive abilities. He had a good understanding when spoken to in English, but had difficulty verbalizing his own thoughts and feelings and ideas in English. He must have had some formal education, because he was really good at basic math and was able to read Spanish print.

More importantly, Grandpa never learned to drive, never applied for a license. He never owned a car. He walked everywhere he went.

This turned out to be a blessing in disguise. Because he walked everywhere in this small town, people easily got to meet and know him. They would see him everywhere: walking to the store, walking to the park, walking to church, to work. He quickly became a staple figure -- someone whom everybody knew and recognized. They accepted that he did not speak English, and they nevertheless always gave him a friendly greeting. They would acknowledge him in English with “Hey, Jesus!” “Morning, Jesus!” “How’s it going, Jesus?” The townspeople liked Grandpa. They also liked calling him Jesus.

Grandma and Grandpa loved their new life and their new environment. They began to build a family. They were home!

Mom once told me about a tragic accident that occurred when she was only a child. One day, Grandpa came home from work at the foundry. There had been an accident, and he had gotten his hands tangled up in one of the machines. A few of his fingers, on both hands, were mangled and a few were hanging, partially severed. When he got to the house, his hands were wrapped in bloody, work towels. When Grandma unraveled the cloth, she could see the serious damage to his fingers. She gave him whisky to drink, cleaned his fingers with rubbing alcohol, and sutured what fingers she could salvage. Two fingers had to be severed. She did this as quickly as she could, knowing how painful it was to Grandpa.

They did not have any health insurance, and they were convinced that a doctor would cost too much. They had saved enough money over the years, but Grandma was confident that she could treat him without a doctor. Grandpa agreed and endured the pain as she stitched him up and then swabbed his hands with iodine. Their only concern at this time was if and when Grandpa would be able to go back to work.

One week later, Grandpa and a bi-lingual co-worker went to speak to their boss. They told him Grandpa was ready to go back to work. Their boss was sympathetic and told Grandpa he could work in a different position that did not require the hand dexterity of his previous job. In addition, the new position paid slightly more.

"America is a great country!" Grandpa said so.

Grandpa was happy with his new job. Grandma was happy too. He continued the part-time railroad job for several more years until he was laid off due to the Depression in the 30s. Nevertheless, life was great. Even grandma's pet parrot, Tarzan, was excited. The parrot had mostly green and a few yellow feathers, and some red ones around his neck and chest. Every time he was hungry or thirsty, he would loudly call out "Grandma" or "Grandpa". And they would always see to his needs.

I was born in Texas. My parents had moved there once they became adults and didn't want to live through another harsh Nebraska winter. Grandpa wouldn't move. He told them that he would never set foot in Texas. He used some graphic words to describe Texans, and they weren't flattering. He and grandma never left their little Nebraska hamlet.

When I was about age five, my parents temporarily separated, for reasons of their own. They decided that I should go live with Grandpa and Grandma until things got better at home. Mom and I boarded a train and headed for Nebraska. Mom stayed a few days with us and then went back to Texas. So there I was in Nebraska with Grandma and Grandpa and their pet parrot, Tarzan, whom they spoiled to no end. At that time Grandma and Grandpa were strangers to me since I had only met them once before.

They were warm and loving caretakers to their ornery grandson. I became very close to the two of them. We only spoke Spanish at home, but I had no problem transitioning to English when at school and in public. These were happy times that I will always cherish. They spoiled me, almost as much as Tarzan.

I too became close to Tarzan. In the back of the house, there was hardly any grass, but the rhubarb grew wild there. Grandpa and I would cut it down several times a year. Grandma would make rhubarb pie and canned rhubarb jam, which she shared with the neighbors. I would feed small pieces of raw rhubarb to Tarzan. He loved his rhubarb more than his regular diet of sunflower seeds. He would often yell "*rubar ...rubar*."

For no particular reason, I once asked Grandpa when he was born. He said he wasn't sure, but that his mother told him he was born when the *calabaza*, a gourd, was ripe. I later discovered that he was born around December, 1895. This date remains an approximation.

About a year after Grandpa's accident, he bought a small plot of land, around two acres. In early spring, I joined him in planting seeds for corn, peppers, watermelon, *calabaza*, and tomatoes. On his days off, we would go out to the *siembra,* or sown field, to maintain the growing vegetables.

Later in the year, at harvest time, he and I often went together to gather the vegetables ripe for harvesting. Grandma would always pack us lunch – white bread with bologna and mustard, and Kool-Aid. (Grandma never drank tap water. She did not like the taste. She made sure she always had plenty of packets of flavored Kool-Aid.) We'd walk to the *siembra*, about three miles from home, and spend the whole day there. Then we'd load the picked vegetables into gunny sacks and carry them home. It was a wonderful thing...growing our own food for consumption; just as the adage says *Living off the land!*

Fast forward to after my tenth birthday. I was happily living with Grandma, Grandpa, and Tarzan. Grandma had been fighting cancer for several years, but she refused to seek proper treatment. In those days, there was little doctors could do with advanced cancer. One day, feeling so much pain, she finally agreed to go to the hospital. Mom had come up from Texas, as did other family members. That night I went to sleep in grandma's bedroom, in her bed, while everyone else, except for one of my aunts, went to the hospital to be with Grandma.

I had already fallen asleep, when I was awakened by Grandma's voice. I sat up and saw her seated at the vanity brushing her long, salt and pepper hair. She looked at me through her reflection in the mirror. In Spanish, she said "Don't worry about me, my love. I no longer have any pain. I am happy and at peace. I am in a wonderful place now. I want you to be happy and not to worry about anything. Take care of your Grandpa. I love you."

I felt safe, secure, and comfortable, so I went back to sleep. I don't know how much later I was awakened by my aunt's voice. Again I sat up, and she was standing in the doorway.

"Tommy, your Grandma has gone to be with the Lord. She died about an hour ago" she said.

"I know" I replied. And I went back to sleep.

Now, Grandpa was alone...with me and Tarzan... but only for a short time. After some discussion, Mom decided that I would go back to Texas with her because Grandpa wanted to be alone. He was still working and didn't want to be solely responsible for my welfare. I didn't want to go to Texas, but I had no choice. I was only ten, and I wanted to be with Grandpa - to comfort him. I reluctantly went back to Texas with Mom. I didn't want to leave Grandpa, and I certainly didn't want to go to Texas because of what Grandpa had said had happened to him and Grandma when they were there. But a 10 year-old has to obey what adults decide is right for him. I was a little defiant, but it turned out to be okay. I adjusted and adapted.

On the drive to Texas, I told Mom about Grandma's visit the night she died. Mom said that I was having a dream. I insisted that it was not a dream.

"I saw her and she talked to me. I was awake."

Mom looked at me from the rear view mirror. "What you saw and heard was Grandma's soul. Grandma died, but her soul lives on. The soul never dies; only the body."

I did not fully understand her explanation. Grandma's visit was very real.

For years after that, I did not see much of Grandpa. At age 21 and a college graduate, I wanted to spend some of that first summer at Grandpa's house. The drive to Nebraska was about 12 hours. Solo, I was able to do it in one day. It was a nice break from home and school. In a sense, Grandpa's house seemed more like home to me than the house in Texas.

Grandpa had retired and was glad to have me for company, now. He was missing Grandma more than ever and was feeling lonely. Even Tarzan had died, from old age I suspect. But Grandpa said it was because he really missed Grandma. Tarzan's feathers had turned grey, and he hardly ever made a sound, not even for rhubarb. One day, Grandpa found Tarzan lying on the bottom of the large, wire cage -- dead. He decided to bury him out back where the wild rhubarb grew. He dug a large hole and set the entire cage with Tarzan still in it into the ground. He covered it with dirt and lime stone to mark the spot. He said a little prayer over the grave. RIP, Tarzan!

Grandpa watched a lot of TV. He had an old black and white console. He never owned a color TV. I thought it strange that he was into daytime soap operas. He knew all the characters and their "nasty" habits and affairs. I would laugh when he would call out a character "You lie!"; "You cheat!"; "You no goot!" And he would say in broken English "He no likie" or "She no lova heem."

Another unexpected change in Grandpa was that he had become a Jehovah's Witness. He said that one day these two young men came to his door and offered him Religious magazines in Spanish: *Despertad* (Awake) and *La Atalaya* (The Watchtower). He gave them a small donation and read the magazines. Although raised a Catholic, he had no issue with becoming a Jehovah's Witness. The young men returned a few months later, and Grandpa gave them more money and they gave him a 10-year subscription to both magazines. Thus began Grandpa's interest in and return to a religious life.

"But, Grandpa" I said. "You were raised a Catholic, and you were even an altar boy at the little church in your pueblo back in Mexico. I was raised Catholic in Texas and I also was an altar boy just like you. I don't understand this change in your religion. I think it's wrong."

He smiled and said in Spanish "I believe in God and in Jesus Christ. But religion has little to do with those beliefs. Religions are what man has created. God is God and always is God. One's 'religion' doesn't really matter that much." Years later, I would again try to understand his message: so many men – so many religions; only one God. It's all good!

One day Grandpa and I were walking to the Woolworth to pick up some supplies, and, as usual, people were greeting him familiarly.

"Who's the boy, Jesus?"

"I'm his grandson, Thomas" I would interject. Letting them know that I spoke and understood English.

Outside the Woolworth's, a woman approached us and in a kindly manner said "I know everybody calls you Jesus, Mr. Ramirez. But your name in English is Jesse. You should not go by the name Jesus. I don't think God likes that. Out of respect for Our Lord, you should say your name is Jesse. And people should call you Jesse. You know! Like Jesse James."

Grandpa had never heard this before, and he certainly was not going to correct what people wanted to call him. He smiled and took the lady's advice in good faith. He never had a quarrel with the townspeople. He accepted them at face value, as they did him.

He stood out in this almost totally white community. Grandpa was dark-skinned with indigenous features. And yet, he never felt out of place or "foreign" or alien. That's why he never became a citizen of the USA. He felt comfortable with his place in the community. He felt accepted. And, his citizenship was never questioned.

Grandpa had seen the TV series "The Legend of Jesse James" a few years earlier. But it never occurred to him that his name in English was Jesse.

The name 'Jesse' stayed on his mind. That Friday we were watching TV and a movie about Jesse James came on. It was an old movie from 1939 simply titled "Jesse James".

I told Grandpa "If you had a color TV, we could watch this movie in color."

Grandpa said he was used to his old black and white TV, and that he did not need a new color TV. He liked Tyrone Power, the actor who played Jesse James.

After the movie, he talked about how much he admired this guy Jesse James. He believed that Jesse James was not a bad guy, the Robin Hood of the Mid-West. He reminded me that one of his neighbors was named James Zorn, and that people called him Jim. So Grandpa decided that Jesse James should be called Jesse Jim. After all, he was now beginning to feel very familiar with Jesse James.

The following week, I went to the library to gather some information on Jesse James. The librarian was very helpful, and we found a black and white picture of Mr. James, and his brother Frank. She made me a copy of Jesse's photo. I took it to the Woolworth's and had it framed and wrapped.

I brought the package home and said "Grandpa, I got you a gift." He opened it, and his eyes widened.

"Is this Jesse Jim?" he asked.

"Yes. That's the real Jesse" I said. "Not a TV actor."

We hung the picture on the living room wall near the TV set. That way Grandpa could look at it all the time. He would often point to it and say "Jesse Jim." I would echo him like Tarzan might have, if he were still alive. "That's right, Grandpa. Jesse Jim."

I spent a little over a month with Grandpa, watching soap operas and old movies on his black and white TV. Sometimes I would page through his J. W. magazines. I was never bored because we talked a lot. He had sold the *siembra*, and had a small pension and social security as income. He was doing okay, except he was missing grandma and having short-term memory problems. I was aware of this. Yet, he told me one day, in Spanish, "I know I'm smarter now than I used to be, but I just have a hard time proving it these days. My memory is stubborn."

I returned to Texas at the end of summer to prepare for graduate school. Mom occasionally kept me informed as to Grandpa's status. She would call him every Sunday. He never complained and never had anything negative to say. He kept busy doing his own cooking and cleaning. Mom was now able to fly up to see him at least three or four times a year, including his birthday and holidays. During her visits, her biggest task was doing his laundry. He did not like doing laundry and usually had several fully loaded hampers. She said he always asked about me. He missed the family, but insisted on staying alone up north, watching soaps and reading his magazines.

More than five years would pass when one mid-December morning, Mom got a call. It was from Jim Zorn, Grandpa's neighbor. He had been trying to contact Grandpa, who had not answered the phone or the door bell. So Jim shook open the back door and went in. He found Grandpa deceased in his bed. It appeared he had died in his sleep. Mom was very upset, but she had been preparing for this moment for a long time. Grandpa was about 83 years old. He never mentioned any health problems. He seemed to be content, living his life his way as best he could.

Arrangements were made, and we all managed to make it to Nebraska for the wake and funeral. Mom, Dad, and I went in one car. The drive north was quiet and tranquil. One might say peaceful. My parents and I were silent and into our own private thoughts of Grandpa. The only sound was that of the car heater buzzing and hissing.

Grandpa's obituary in the local paper read "Entered into Eternal Rest". I thought that was beautiful. The wake was held for one night in the living room of his house, with open casket. Many of the neighbors, friends, and family came from Texas, including my aunts and uncles from Kansas City and surrounding areas in Nebraska.

I remember going up to the casket and looking down at Grandpa's hands -- one resting on the other, stubs for fingers, and that waxy skin appearance. His face was relaxed, and yet, I detected a subtle grin. So I grinned too. He looked worry-free and content, as he should be.

After the funeral and burial, we had the task of closing out the house and putting it up for sale. I suppose we were in the stages of both closure and grief. Going through Grandpa's things, I came across some papers in an old and grease-spotted manila envelope. It contained two U. S. Department of Labor manifests with Grandma and Grandpa's names.

Green cards, or Permanent Resident Cards, were not introduced until 1950 as a result of the Alien Registration Act of 1940. The manifests were stamped May 15, 1917. No wonder Grandpa thought Nebraska was beautiful. It was spring in Nebraska when he decided to settle there. He had not yet experienced a winter. Nevertheless, not even the winters that followed could dissuade him from enduring life in this plain and sometimes desolate place. He learned to welcome the change of seasons.

Images of my grandparents passing through customs and immigration at the Texas-Mexican border came to me. They were so young and courageous to have left their warm and familiar village in Mexico to venture into a very different and unfamiliar land, not speaking the language and not knowing what the future may bring; hanging onto the strings of hope. Grandpa wanted to have a better life for himself and his young bride, and had the foresight to consider his offspring...children and grandchildren. He wanted a better life for all of us. It was a little like the Europeans who came through Ellis Island. The difference being, there was no Statue of Liberty at the Rio Grande border. And yet, the American Dream was not just a slogan or a myth to Grandpa. It was an aspiration.

When I hear people say they are proud to be American, it makes me a little vexed. I can understand their perspective. But I think of pride as a result of having accomplished something. I'm proud of earning my graduate degree. I had little to do with being born in this country. Nevertheless, I'm happy and extremely grateful to be an American. I appreciate being American and all that it represents. And I am proud of America because of its accomplishments.

Grandpa was proud of having made it to America. He took pride in what he had accomplished. He did not let his experience in Texas stand in the way of achieving his dream. And I am also grateful to him for having succeeded where many had failed, so that his descendents might be here in America and perhaps have a better life. In fact, I owe him my very existence here in America. I have an attitude of enormous gratitude.

Our family decided to stay in Nebraska for Christmas before heading back to Texas for the New Year. It seemed the right thing to do. We celebrated both Christmas, the birth of Jesus, and Grandpa's life. Amid smiles and tears, we toasted Grandpa and Grandma. I also toasted the picture of Jesse Jim on the wall.

My last night there, lying alone in Grandma's bed, I thought of my grandparents and all they had done for me and for the family. I whispered to them *I love you, Grandma. I love you, Grandpa. Thank you, Grandma! Thank you, Grandpa. And thank you, Jēsus!*

www.uscis.gov

Introduction

There are people in our lives who stay in our minds and memories, for better or for worse. They made an impression on us. It's not easy, but it's best to separate the negative memories from the positive ones. Hold on to the positive ones.

Children are usually very good at observing the behavior of adults, and they look forward to adulthood. They sometimes want to be adults more than the adults want them to be adults. But there is no stopping maturity and development. People and things grow.

Some of us were fortunate enough to have good role models. Maybe not paragons of excellence, but just good people – compassionate and caring.

Most doctors and nurses are like that. Most helping professionals – social workers, psychologists, care givers, etc. – are like that. We desperately need more people like them.

Similarly are law enforcement representatives and the military. They are held to a higher standard and are expected to serve and protect the rest of us. That is a lot of responsibility.

I thank them all. I thank the doctor (and others like him) in this story. He made a positive difference in one boy's life.

Dr. Zamora

"Ah! Happy years! Once more,
who would not be a boy?

Lord Byron

"In nothing do men more nearly approach the gods
than in giving health to men".
Cicero, *Pro Ligario*

The boy and his dad stood admiring the family's 1956 Pontiac, which was sitting innocently in the driveway. It was a beautiful two-tone, green and beige, four-door sedan and was nearly 10 years old. The boy, not quite old enough (at age 14) to drivc, was excited and eager to get behind the green steering wheel and pretend the big machine was his to drive. But his mission this Saturday morning was not to drive, but to help his dad. The car had a flat rear tire. They would replace that old flat tire with a good tire; and then fix the flat one.

The boy's dad started the job, but the boy interrupted him, insisting that he be allowed to do it. Allowing it with hesitation, his dad reluctantly stood back. Sliding the old iron jack under the rear bumper was no problem for the boy. Pumping the jack up to raise the back end of the car was a bit more difficult. The jack was old and rusty. But there was something very adult about doing this kind of job that made the boy feel manly, grown-up. The act of jacking up the car was itself very manly. The boy felt important, and useful.

Suddenly, without warning, it happened. The jack slipped out from under the rear bumper, and the iron arm of the jack came shooting up into the boys face. It struck him center, under the chin and knocked him back onto his butt. He sat there for a few seconds, stunned, in shock, and a little confused. His dad quickly came to his side and grabbed him.

"Are you okay?" he asked.

"Yes; I think so."

The boy felt no pain, except for numbness under his chin and mouth and around the whole bottom of his face. The boy then began to feel moisture on his chest. His dad was the first to notice the blood. He grabbed a greasy work cloth and held it under the boy's chin.

"Damn it" he said, "you're bleeding all over the place." He peeked below the greasy work cloth. "Looks like you're going to need some stitches. Damn it! I better get you over to see Dr. Zamora. I'm sure he's in his office today." Even if it was Saturday.

They didn't want to waste time calling, so instead, they just got into the old Chevy pickup parked on the street. The boy climbed into the passenger side. He liked riding shot-gun (because he liked the word) and his dad started the engine, slammed the clutch down and put the four-on-the floor in first gear. They could barely hear the boy's mother calling out loudly from the garage door "Que paso? What happened? What happened?"

No time to stop and explain. They needed to get to Dr. Zamora's office right away, as the bleeding would not stop. "Call Dr. Zamora's office! Tell him we have to see him right away!" his dad yelled. They sped off in that old candy-apple red Chevy truck, with its loud muffler.

The office of Dr. Zamora was not far from their home -- about a 10-minute drive. It was just off the Boulevard, next to the Safeway supermarket. To their relief, not only was Dr. Zamora in, but his office parking lot was already filled with cars, including the good doctor's car. It was a small parking lot with only about 5 spaces. So the boy's dad parked the pick-up on the street. He rushed the boy into the reception room, holding a different greasy work cloth under his chin to prevent any more of the blood from spreading. The other patients in the waiting room just stared and whispered to each other. "What happened to that boy....must have fallen. *Que lástima*!" The boy and his dad came up to the receptionist's counter.

"My boy just had an accident and split his chin open. Can the doctor see him right away?" his dad whispered nervously to the receptionist, not wanting to sound too insisting or demanding or cause any disruption. The lady in the wheelchair behind the reception counter said "Sure. Yes, I just talked to your wife, Mr. Lopez. And look at you, young man! Don't worry. You'll be just fine in a few minutes." She looked kindly, gently at the boy. She knew the boy and his dad from previous visits. She was familiar with the family. "I'll buzz him right now. Just have a seat."

Dr. Zamora had opened his office - his family practice - about 10 years earlier. This was a predominately Hispanic neighborhood, mostly Mexican Americans. Fortunately, Dr. Zamora spoke perfect Spanish, as well as acceptable, but with accented, English. The family knew Dr. Zamora because he had been treating the dad's mother, Sra. Celia, for several years. In those days, doctors often made house calls. And when *Dona* Celia was feeling ill or thinking that she was going to die, the family would call Dr. Zamora, and within an hour or two, he would arrive at the home to tend to grandma, *Dona* Celia. Often, it was a "cry wolf" or “the sky is falling” situation, with *Dona* Celia, just wanting some attention, and especially Dr. Zamora’s attention. You see, Dr. Zamora, although a medical doctor, had the “gift” of making people laugh. He used to say “When my patients smile, they start to feel better.” This was one of his “intended” prescriptions. He would always say and do things to make his patients laugh, or at least smile, which seemed to help their medical conditions. He felt that laughter was a very effective medicine to be used as treatment, not a cure. So when he would arrive at their home and find *Dona* Celia grimacing in pain and complaining about how bad she is feeling, Dr. Zamora would say something cute, like "*Dona* Celia, did you have too much tequila last night again? I have told you to stay off that stuff!" And Grandma Celia would start to laugh, and within a few minutes she was feeling much better, her ailment subsiding. But of course, Dr. Zamora had to give her something to validate her "feeling so bad". So, it was aspirin or her standard insulin dose. This was more of a placebo than a curative treatment.

The boy often gave his grandma her insulin injections himself. He liked doing this because it made him feel like he was Dr. Zamora.

A few years later, before grandma Celia eventually did pass on, while in the hospital, the parish priest and Dr. Zamora were there for her. The priest gave last rites and walked out of the room with the good doctor. The boy remembered that, as he was sitting in the hospital waiting area he overheard Dr. Zamora say to the good priest "I don't think heaven is ready for her, Father". And the boy had laughed quietly, while wiping a tear from his cheek.

On another occasion, Dr. Zamora got into a political argument with one of his patients. The patient was telling Dr. Zamora that his candidate was more qualified than the good doctor's candidate. Dr. Zamora said that he did not like talking politics or religion, because it always ends up becoming a moot point and turns into an argument. The patient said that there was no argument, because he was right, and anyone supporting the other candidate was wrong.

Dr. Zamora smiled and said "Juan, in a sense, you are right. You see, there is a Chinese saying that an argument is when the goal is to find out who is right! A discussion, on the other hand, is when the goal is to find out what is right! In politics and religion, there is always an argument; almost never a discussion. People feel very strongly about those issues. Those topics are emotional and personal. And that's why I avoid them."

Juan just shook his head and said "Chinese? You've got to be kidding, doc! The Chinese don't know anything about us Americans. Anyway, maybe the Chinese are wrong." And so, it had, ultimately, become a moot point. With that, Juan gave up his argument, and chose to take a more conservative path; careful not to aggravate or agitate Dr. Zamora, lest his physical exam take an unpleasant turn. Dr. Zamora was treating him for chronic, severe hemorrhoids.

Not being from the around here, people of the neighborhood had been curious about Dr. Zamora and his origins. He was not very tall and slightly overweight. His skin was dark, and he had very white teeth. He sometimes referred to himself as the Mexican Puerto Rican doctor. People weren't sure if he was Mexican American or Mexican or Puerto Rican or whether he had one Mexican parent and one Puerto Rican parent. This was a very curious matter to the people of the neighborhood. But, they never brought up the issue to Dr. Zamora, at least not to his face. Most thought *who cares what he is?* Nevertheless, they still talked about it in private.

One day the boy was curious as to the Doctor's age. It had become common knowledge that Dr. Zamora was born on February 29; year unknown. Dr. Z. would jokingly tell folks that he became a doctor around his 7th birthday. Curious, the boy had asked one of his teachers at school what made Dr. Zamora's birthday so different; and if it was really true that he became a doctor when he was seven years old. She told him that February 29 is an intercalary day or year, meaning that it only occurs every four years, in a Leap year. She further explained that a person born on February 29 is sometimes referred to as a 'bissextile', because in the Julian calendar, February 29 is referred to as the 'bissextus'. The boy found this revelation somewhat disturbing. Dr. Zamora was a 'bissextile'? And even stranger, Dr. Zamora's birthday only came up every four years? His teacher explained that a person born on February 29 could celebrate their birthday "every year" either on February 28 or March 1. The boy had planned to ask Dr. Zamora on which day he celebrated his birthday. But, he never got around to it.

And then there was the matter of the Dr.'s wife. When Dr. Zamora and his new bride first came to the neighborhood, no one knew that she, Nancy, was his wife. She was his nurse and receptionist at the doctor's office. There were just the two of them in the office, and Dr. Zamora never called her by her name. When he needed something, he would just call out "Nurse." It was a small practice, a modest, free-standing building with three exam rooms, and five parking spaces, including one for Dr. Zamora's car. The people of the neighborhood did not find out that Nancy was Dr. Zamora's wife until soon after the accident.

Nancy was an attractive young woman with wavy blond hair, twinkling blue eyes, and with pale satin skin. She was very refined, and people said that she was "sweet". She was always polite and friendly to the people in the neighborhood. But no one knew where she lived or how she became the Mexican Puerto Rican doctor's nurse and receptionist, in an office located in a Latino neighborhood, in the barrio. No matter! The people liked and appreciated this gentle white woman who greeted them at the doctor's office, and always made them feel welcome.

About two years after the doctor's office opened, the good doctor and his good wife, nurse and receptionist, decided to drive the 60 plus miles out of town to visit Nancy's parents' home. The neighborhood later learned that on their return, Dr. Zamora was driving, making jokes about his patients -- in a good sort of way -- when a large truck heading in the opposite direction crossed the center lane and hit them head-on. The driver of the truck, a good Christian man, had been driving for almost 14 hours without rest or sleep. In the accident, Nancy suffered a spinal cord injury that left her paralyzed from the waist down. Dr. Zamora, miraculously, emerged with only some ugly bruises and a broken arm.

Less than two months later, both were back to work at the office. The only difference was that Nancy was now confined to a wheelchair. The office was remodeled to accommodate the wheelchair. Nancy wanted to stay on as nurse and receptionist. It was after the accident that people learned that Nancy and Dr. Zamora were husband and wife. The people were saddened by this incident, and many had mixed feelings. Some people, as is often the case, wanted to blame someone for the accident; some even wanted to blame Dr. Zamora. Some said that Dr. Zamora should have been the one injured more seriously, after all "he charges too much." The women of the neighborhood were sad because this meant that as a result of the accident, Nancy and Dr. Zamora might never have children; short of adoption. They thought "What a tragedy! She...so young and beautiful... and not able to have children. May God bless them both!"

Over the years, Dr. Zamora's practice grew, and soon he discovered that he needed to be open six days a week, and be on call every day. He hired another nurse, Ms. Alvarez, fresh out of nursing school, but

Nancy continued as the full time nurse, part time receptionist, and the one with the most administrative responsibilities. Now, nearly 8 years later, they had put the accident, the tragedy, behind them and focused on serving their patients. There was work to be done. No time for regrets or ruminations. And, most importantly, it seemed that the love between Dr. Zamora and his wife Nancy grew stronger and tighter. This was the most positive and most meaningful thing to come from the accident.

And so on this Saturday, the boy and his dad found themselves sitting in the waiting room of Dr. Zamora's office. Within minutes of Nancy's call to the doctor, he entered the waiting room and motioned the boy and his dad to follow him to one of the exam rooms in the back. Dr. Zamora turned to Nancy and said "Nurse, tell the others waiting that I have an emergency and they'll have to wait a few more minutes. And, oh yes, sanitize one of my surgical knives. I'm going to need it for this boy!" Of course, the boy did not know that Dr. Zamora was just joking. The boy got very nervous! *A surgical knife? A scalpel?* The boy's dad said "He's only kidding, son. You know how Dr. Zamora is." The boy and his dad followed the good doctor to a back room. The boy was made to sit on the end of the doctor's examination table.

"Okay" he said, "let's see what we have here." He removed the greasy work cloth, now a blood-soaked rag, and carefully scrutinized the gash under the boy's chin. "Hmmm. Well, I think you are going to need a few stitches to close that thing up." Dr. Zamora started opening cabinets and drawers. He seemed frustrated. He could not find what he was looking for.

"Nurse", he called to his wife, Nancy.

"Yes, Doctor." She rolled her wheelchair into the room.

"Where's the anesthetic? I can't find any. I hope we aren't out of it."

"Sorry, doctor! I told you this morning that I had ordered anesthetics, alcohol, and other medical supplies yesterday, and they were supposed to be here this morning, but they are yet to be delivered. I called, and they should be here sometime today. Nurse Alvarez was supposed to stop at the drugstore to pick up some alcohol, but, as you know, she was unable to come in today."

"Great!" he said disgustingly. "Well, I guess we'll just have to do the stitching without anesthesia. Thank goodness I at least have some rubbing alcohol," he said seriously.

The boy's dad smiled, and he turned to the boy and said, "He's only kidding. You know how the good doctor is." The boy was only temporarily relieved.

"Oh, no," said Dr. Zamora. "I'm not kidding. I don't have any Novocain or other anesthetic; all I have is a little rubbing alcohol. It will have to do. But I can't use too much. I don't know if I will have enough to last until those supplies get here."

The boy, no longer relieved or relaxed, said nothing. The room became quite and serious. Dr. Zamora had the boy sit straight, upright, chin up, and proceeded to clean the wound with alcohol and gauze. He then prepared a needle and black thread.

"You look like a brave and tough boy. You are a tough young man, aren't you?" The boy nodded. "I think you can handle this. Think of some jokes your friends tell you or a TV show that made you laugh, and you won't feel a thing." But of course, the boy could not think of any jokes or any TV episodes, except a little of "The Rifleman". Instead, the boy was focused on the needle entering the skin of his chin. The doctor gently leaned the boy's head back, and the boy stared up at the ceiling.

Then he felt the sting, followed by the pulling of the thread...one stitch, two stitches....

That is when Dr. Zamora started telling him this story: "You know, last night, Friday night, late, this guy comes in to the office just as we were about to leave for the day. His wife brought him in. He was stone drunk. And, he stunk to high heaven of booze and cigarette smoke. I know the guy and his family. He's usually a pretty nice fellow. His problem is he just drinks a little too much. That wouldn't be so bad, except that he does not know how to hold his liquor, and the booze makes him violent. That's usually a sign of underlying anger and frustration due to other things going on in his life.

"Anyway, he had been at that bar down by the railroad tracks, and he got into a fight with two other guys. One of them hit him over the head with a bottle and opened up quite a gash. Then the other guy hit him just above his left eye with a beer can, giving him another gash. Well, this poor fella had a lot of bleeding, both from the gash on the back of his head and the gash just above the eye. If the beer can had hit him just an eighth of an inch lower, he probably would have lost that eye. Well, I say to Nancy, 'Nurse, get me the stitching kit and some anesthetic'. I bring the guy back here, and he sat down right here, where you are sitting. And I stop the bleeding with gauze and a little alcohol. My nurse comes in and says 'Doctor, I'm so sorry. Give me a few minutes, and I'll dig some anesthetic up from the supply closet.'

"As she turned around in her chair, she said 'We have plenty of rubbing alcohol'. Well, I tell the bloody man that we'll have to wait for the anesthetic. 'It won't take long', I assure him. Well, the guy looks up at me. Blurry and wet eyed, and slurring, he says 'No need, doc. I don't need no alcohol or any of that "anatheeza" stuff. Just sew me up and let me be on my way.'"

The boy listened intently; his mind focused only on the story.

“Well, with nothing to numb the wound, I first stitched the back of his head. He never made a sound and never moved. Then I started on the gash over his eye. Well, do you know what? I stitched up this guy with just a few dabs of alcohol. And do you know that as I was pulling the thread just above his eye ... Why this guy, he never even flicked an eye lash! He just sat there with this stupid grin on his face. He never said a word. I tied and knotted the last stitch and told him I was done. He said 'Thanks, doc. How much?' I charged him $19.50. I took off $.50 cents since I didn't use an anesthetic. Never flicked an eye lash, that guy; never even winced. Go figure! Must have been the booze! He walked out of here a happy camper. And he refused pain medication. So I asked him ‘didn’t you feel any pain?’ And the guy says ‘No, doc. I was praying the whole time and didn’t feel a thing.’ Praying seemed to help him with the pain. Unfortunately, I’m neither authorized nor qualified to prescribe prayer."

Dr. Zamora told the boy this story the whole time he was quickly stitching his chin. The boy was so engrossed and so focused on listening to the story that he never felt the needle go in and out of his chin. In fact, by the end of the story, Dr. Zamora was done stitching, and the boy was smiling. And so was his dad.

"It's going to feel numb, and it will itch for a day or two, and the swelling will last for about 24 hours, but it will pass. Put an ice pack on it when you get home. Make an appointment with my nurse to come back on Tuesday, and I'll check the stitches. You’re young, so you should heal pretty quickly. The stitches should be ready to come out by then. Do you have any questions?"

"No, doc! I think we can handle it from here", the boy’s dad said.

"By the way, how did this happen?"

The boy perked up and interjected "I was replacing a tire on the Pontiac."

Dr. Zamora turned to the boy's dad, laughing "Hopefully, he'll be more careful next time. Maybe auto mechanics is not his thing. Your dad tells me you're an altar boy at a church nearby."

"Yes, I am. Were you an altar boy?" the boy queried.

"No. I'm not a Catholic. But I am a Christian."

The boy did not understand this explanation. How could someone not be a Catholic and yet be a Christian? Someone else would have to explain it, but not now. He just wanted to get out of the good Doctor's office and go home.

"He's a really dedicated altar boy." His father added. "Once he served three masses in one day; including a wedding. I'm very proud of him."

"And so you should be." said Dr. Zamora.

After leaving the exam room, the boy's dad paid cash for the service and firmed their Tuesday appointment. The boy and his dad were escorted to the door by Dr. Zamora himself.

"I'll be with you folks in a second" the doctor said to the patients anxiously waiting to see him. The boy's dad said, half serious, "You really need to do something about the parking situation here, Doc. I had to park on the street because all of your parking spaces were taken."

The good doctor looked at the boy's dad and said "What are you talking about, Lopez? No parking spaces." He opened the door and pointed to the Safeway across his lot, and at the supermarket's many parking spaces. "There's my parking lot. Plenty of parking spaces. How many spaces do you need?" The boy laughed, even though it made his face hurt a little.

“See you guys in a few days.” And as the door closed behind them, the boy and his dad could hear Dr. Zamora call out “Nurse!”

* * * * *

To this day, over 50 years later, now a grown man, he remembers that visit to the office of Dr. Zamora. There is only a small scar under his chin now; hardly noticeable. But it remains there as a reminder of that painless "operation". He thinks of the old Pontiac, the rusty jack, and the accidents -- his accident and Dr. Zamora and Nancy's accident.

He ponders his injury and Nancy's injury. And he realizes how fortunate he was then, and still is. How blessed he was, back then, to have had his dad, his mom, Grandma Celia, and of course, Dr. Zamora and Nurse Nancy! All deceased now. He sometimes says a little prayer for them, assured that they are all together in Heaven. They were good people.

Introduction

Often, there are a lot of characters in a story. Each character deserves recognition, but this is a difficult order when writing a short story, as compared to a novel. I have done my best to write about a few characters who were close for a while, but whose legacy lives on.

That sense of belonging is very important to young people. Maybe that is why so many join clubs and organizations. Whether it's an athletic team, a cheering squad, a fraternity or sorority, the school band, or the debate club, the goal is to be a part of something; to be included in something. Let it be said that this also adds structure to a young person's life.

And so it was with the Altar boys ... and the Boy Scouts.

A Leader of Boy Scouts

"The final test of a leader is that he leaves behind him in other men the conviction and they will to carry on."

Walter Lippmann

Javier (Javi) was big. At 55 years of age, he was 6' tall and weighed nearly 300 pounds. He was overweight, sloppy, lazy, and he liked "the bottle". He never finished high school and had been married for 30 years, yet he and his wife had no children. We never mentioned it in his presence, but most of us boys in the Boy Scout troop were convinced that he was sterile, and that too much tequila had caused it. A veteran, he had been wounded in combat. People who knew him said he had depression, and quietly suspected PTSD. But he dismissed it all as "nonsense".

Javier was our Boy Scout Troop Leader, Unit Leader, and Scoutmaster. This meant that he would oversee a meeting twice each month with members of troop Council #365. He would also arrange for various annual Boy Scout functions in the region, and state-wide, like Jamboree. He made sure the boys had uniforms and supplies and equipment for various activities and events. Although he only worked part-time at the stockyards, much of the funding for the council came out of his own pocket. He was aware that most of the boys could not afford the dues and other costs. His wife was not too pleased with this because she worked full-time and was, in effect, the primary money earner for the two of them.

Javier was a kind man. He did not talk a lot, except when intoxicated, and was not a typical leader, and not a very good disciplinarian. Nevertheless, he was liked by his boys, and we felt a kinship to him. He was easy on us, and sometimes funny. He idolized famous entertainers like Cantinflas and Charlie Chaplin. (Cantinflas was sometimes referred to as the Mexican Charlie Chaplin.) He would imitate Chaplin and sometimes walk like him, with a tree branch for a cane, just to make the boys laugh. He looked funny because his body was nothing like Chaplin's. Sometimes, he would even wear a little fake mustache like Chaplin's.

The boys were a motley group. There was Robert, "Stick". Stick was skinny and always carried a measuring tape with him. He would measure everything. Why? Who knows! But the boys were surprised at how often Stick's measuring tape came in handy.

Then there were the twins, Michael and Daniel. They were a very funny pair, both very overweight, and indistinguishable. They were affectionately called "Slim and Slimmer". Their favorite pastime was watching British movies. They would quote lines with a British accent, from movies. They liked to say the words "murder", but like "muuuuuurrrdah", and "'enry 'iggins". When they were about 5 years old, their mother took them grocery shopping with her. They were difficult to control sometimes, and she would have to yell at them to stop touching the items on the shelves. "Michael...Daniel...over here, please!" One day, a lady came up to her and said "Oh, how cute. You look Hispanic, and you gave your boys Irish names!" Their mother replied. "Irish? Oh, no, miss! Their names are from the Bible." The lady walked away.

Roger, actually, Rogelio; but he did not like the Spanish appellation, was the youngest, and was undoubtedly the smartest of the group. He was shy, polite, friendly, and a bit on the *feminine* side. The boys used to make fun of him because of his physical attributes, but he held his own, so they eventually gave up teasing him and just accepted Roger for being Roger.

Besides, he was more articulate than they (we) were, and he always had the last word in an exchange of retorts.

"Twitchy" was named so because he had one eye that seemed to always blink, twitch; a tic; or spasm. He was also anemic. And, he would always talk badly about his single mother, calling her "overbearing" and "controlling". He was determined to disobey her at every opportunity. He blamed her for not having a father around for him.

Bruce, or Brucie, was the trouble maker. He was always getting into fights, but not with any of his fellow scouts. He had also gotten into trouble at school and had run-ins with the law for stealing things.

Chico was the runt of the group. He was always talking and making jokes and was a great storyteller. But, his babbling was more like background noise to the other boys. We felt sorry for him because he was small of stature and probably couldn't fight his way out of a paper bag.

Me? I'm Chato; so named because of my pug nose. We were the regulars and we were close because we were also altar boys at the same church. There were 9 or 10 other boys who ventured in and out of troop meetings and events. They were not really serious about scouting.

Every meeting would begin with the Pledge of Allegiance, hands on hearts and facing the American flag. We spoke in unison, but often forgetting some of the words. Still, our hearts were in the right place. The meetings always ended with all the boys reciting in chorus the Prayer of St. Francis. I've always loved that prayer and still repeat it today.

Twice a year, Javier would go over the principles of Scouting. He would read them aloud, and we would have to repeat after him.

"Okay, boys! Repeat after me:

'**Scout Oath:** On my honor I will do my best to do my duty to God and my country and to obey the Scout Law; to help other people at all times; to keep myself physically strong, mentally awake, and morally straight.

'**Scout Law:** A Scout is trustworthy, loyal, helpful, friendly, courteous, kind, obedient, cheerful, thrifty, brave, clean, and reverent.

'**Scout Mission:** The mission of the Boy Scouts of America is to prepare young people to make ethical and moral choices over their lifetimes by instilling in them the values of the Scout Oath and Scout Law.'

Thank you, boys! That was very well done. Please don't ever forget the importance of these life-long principles. They are the foundation of the BSA."

In the early summer of 1960, Javier showed up for the meeting, as usual, "intoxicated". He had been drinking and was slurring his speech and walking like his legs were made of rubber. When he tried walking like Chaplin, he nearly fell down. The boys, although somewhat accustomed to his frequent drunken presentations, were nevertheless uncomfortable with this.

"Boys, I have the pleasure of introducing to you an Eagle Scout who just recently moved into this area. He is a fine young man and a credit to the Boy Scouts of America. He is going to assist me this summer in organizing and implementing two field trips. He is experienced and knowledgeable. Jimmy, come on up." He motioned to a figure behind us.

From the back of the room, Jimmy made his way to the front and introduced himself. He was a fine looking young man, well-spoken, and athletic-looking. At 19, he was older than the scouts in the unit, who averaged 12-14 years of age. As an Eagle Scout, he had earned at least 21 merit badges and had been successfully approved by the Review Board for the rank of Eagle Scout. Attending a local community college part-time, he managed to also work at a local country club as a tennis instructor. The boys did not know what a "country club" was, so Jimmy described it to us. It sounded really cool. Jimmy was the perfect role model for us boys.

The first field trip would be into the wooded area outside of town. Jimmy would help us set up the tents and other paraphernalia for the two-night stay. We got written permission from our parents and were very excited for the opportunity to earn some merit badges. Jimmy would also conduct many of the activities, like teaching us to tie knots and build a fireplace. We would leave on a small rented bus with a driver. It would be great!

The first day and night went great. The next day, after lunch, we were all busy doing assigned stuff. Jimmy approached Roger.

"I think you'd appreciate learning about the flora and fauna of the forest. What do ya' think?"

Roger was hesitant, but said "Sure".

The two quietly set out into the woods, with hardly anyone noticing they were gone. Just before dinner, Jimmy and Roger returned. Jimmy seemed really pleased with their venture into the woods; Roger not so much.

"We, Roger and I, learned a lot about flora and fauna. Didn't we Roger?"

With hesitation, Roger said "Yeah. It was really cool. I learned which plants to stay away from. I even learned which plants I can eat." He smiled.

The camping field trip went well. We all enjoyed it and were looking forward to our next field trip, which would be to Lake Alo. At the following meeting, we learned more details about the Lake Alo trip. After the meeting, Roger and I walked together back toward our homes.

"Lake Alo sounds like it's going to be fun", I said.

"I don't think I'm going", Roger replied, tracking his feet on the sidewalk.

"Why not?"

"I've been there before."

"Yeah, but not with other scouts; not with the gang. We'll go swimming and fishing and boating. It'll be fun."

"No. I think I'll pass."

Sensing something wrong, I asked "What's wrong, Roger. You're not acting yourself. I'm your friend. Tell me what's bothering you."

"Well... I don't like that guy, Jimmy. I just don't like him."

"Why? Didn't he take you out into the woods and teach you all about the foliage, the plants and grass and stuff?"

"Yeah! But he did more than that."

"What is it, dude? What are you trying to say?"

"Well, we did stuff. Or rather, he did stuff ... to me."

"Like what? What?"

"He put his hands on me. He touched me. He.... We.... Well, I can't say it."

I suddenly realized what Roger was trying to tell me. He was ashamed of it. But I was glad that he trusted me enough to tell me.

"Roger, you've got to tell someone; a grown-up. He may want to try it again."

"That's why I'm not going. I can't. I just can't."

"Yes! Yes, you can. If you won't tell, I will."

"But who can I tell?"

"Tell Javier. He'll understand. Please, tell Javier."

"That old drunk?" He paused and was silent for a while. "Well, I'll think about it..."

Roger walked away to his house. I was upset because Roger was my friend. No one had a right to do that to him. I wanted to beat up Jimmy, but he was older and bigger than me. Still, I felt I needed to protect Roger.

Two weeks later, at the next meeting, I pulled Roger over to me.

"You tell Javier tonight, or I will."

Javier was tipsy as expected, but nevertheless Roger went up to him after the meeting and asked to speak to him. I stood watching from afar. Then I saw Javier put his hand on Roger's shoulder and seemed to be reassuring him. Roger and I walked home together again.

"What did he say?"

Roger smiled. "He said that for me not to worry; that I would not see Jimmy at any of our get-togethers again. He told me to stay strong; that I was a smart kid and a good kid; and that what happened was not my fault. He said 'nobody messes with my boys', and that made me feel good."

At the next meeting we finalized the field trip to Lake Alo. Javier started the meeting by saying that Jimmy would not be going with us on this trip. "He decided that he needed to work full-time at the country club and would not be able to join us. In fact, he is not sure if he can come back. But we'll manage just fine without him....won't we boys?"

Everybody said "Yeah!"

I looked over at Roger, and he had a big grin on his face.

The day finally came for the Lake Alo trip. The same rented bus and driver picked us up, and off we went for a two-night trip. Our parents waved good-bye to us. Even Javier's wife was there for the send-off.

It was a beautiful area, the lake, the hills, the foliage. The weather forecast was partly cloudy, humid, with a high about 90 degrees; great weather for swimming in the lake. As soon as we got unpacked and finished setting up the tents, we donned our swim shorts and ran with abandonment to the lake and jumped into nature's cool waters. It was glorious!

There were more than 100 merit badges, and we all wanted to earn a merit badge in Swimming. Privately, I wanted to earn a merit badge in Horsemanship. Splashing and diving, we all enjoyed the lake. Javier watched from shore, every now and then sipping from a cup, which we assumed contained some degree of alcohol. But, no matter; we were having a good time.

The weather in this area is unpredictable. Even forecasters get frustrated. They always include "a chance of" something or other. Sudden changes in the climate/weather are not uncommon. On this day, what started out to be a typical hot, humid summer day, suddenly changed! A thunderstorm rolled in, and it began to rain, dark clouds formed, and the wind picked up. The water became rough and colder. Even I could feel the undertow. Lightning broke through the sky and clouds. We all anxiously began to swim back to shore.

I noticed Stick went under water, came back up, and went under again. He seemed to be struggling to catch his breath. I panicked. I yelled "Mr. Javier! Mr. Javier. Help! It's Stick!" Soon, the other boys were yelling for Mr. Javier.

Javier finally noticed our calls for help. He looked out at us, and we pointed to where Stick was splashing in the water. Javier quickly pulled off his clothes. He did not have swim shorts, just his briefs. *It was not a pretty sight.* He ran as fast as he could, jumped into the water and began swimming toward Stick. I was surprised at how fast this chubby, awkward man could swim. He was at Stick's side in no time. He hugged Stick and pulled him along as he swam back to shore, in the heavy rain and wind, and rough waters.

Once on shore, Javier began to administer artificial respiration to get Stick to breathe and expel the water in his lungs. He seemed to know exactly what to do. After about a minute, Stick began to cough and gag. Javier turned him on his side. Stick seemed to have recovered, and his breathing got better, in spite of his coughing up lake water.

Javier told us boys to stay put and do nothing until he returned. He got the driver to take him and Stick into town, about 45 minutes away. They took Stick to the hospital emergency room. There, Javier contacted Stick's parents and told them what happened. He and the driver then returned to the campsite. We gathered up all the gear, got back on the bus and headed home. That was the shortest field trip ever. But the good news was that Stick was going to be okay. *Thank God! And thanks to Javier!*

I later learned that when Javier got home that evening, he was somewhat shaken. He told his wife what happened. "That boy could've drowned. I would have been responsible."

"You're lucky he didn't. I bet you were drinking. Weren't you?"

Javier held his head down "Yes; a little."

"Javi, you've got to stop drinking. I know you've tried before. But this could have turned out really bad for you, and that boy! It could have been tragic!"

"I know".

Stick totally recovered, and everything seemed to be getting back to normal, when Javier got a knock on his door. It was the local newspaper <u>*and*</u> the local TV reporter. They wanted to interview Javier because they said that he was a Hero who saved a drowning boy's life. They had already interviewed Stick's family, now they wanted to hear what the Hero had to say.

Javier's wife encouraged him to allow the interviews: "Javi, go ahead. It's okay. Tell them your side of the story." So he allowed the interviews. A few days later he got a call from the office of the Mayor. They wanted to give Javi a Hero's Award for Bravery. Javier was taken aback and could not quite understand why all the fuss. Nevertheless, his wife again encouraged him to accept the award and meet with the Mayor.

At the end of that summer, Javier met with the Mayor and City Council members. In front of TV cameras and reporters, he was hardly ready to accept his award. I was present, and Stick was there with his family, as well as the other scouts. It was a proud moment for all of us.

"It is my honor" began the Mayor, "to present this Hero's Award for Bravery to Mr. Javier "Javi" Lopez, a Korean War Veteran and leader of Boy Scouts. Risking his own life, he dove into Lake Alo in the middle of a thunderstorm to save the life of young Robert "Stick" Diaz."

With cameras clicking, Javier accepted his award, framed like a certificate, and looking very authentic. Javier said thank you, and, of course, said that anyone would have done the same. He was shy and humble about the entire matter; a little embarrassed, but still, he allowed himself a little pride.

I was standing next to my parents, and I overheard someone near me say "And I always thought he was just a fat drunk and a loser. I was wrong. He's just a fat drunk". It made me angry when I heard that.

But, Javier's story does not end here. Months later, my mother shared with me the following: On the night of the award presentation, Javier and his wife had a long talk. He told her he was going to stop drinking;

that getting this award meant a lot to him, and that he wanted to change his path in life. He wanted to be a better man, better husband, and a better Scout in life, following Scout values, oath, law, and mission.

"You've made this promise before" his wife said. She was skeptical.

"I know. But this time, I mean it. Really! I want to be a role model to the boys; but I also want to spend more time with you. To do this, I'm going to have to leave the Boy Scouts. I'll also switch to full-time at the stockyards, at least for the next 10 or 12 years before I retire. How does that sound to you?"

"Well, I hate to see you abandon the Scouts, because I know how much that has meant to you and how much you want to lead those boys; and how much you care about them. But, truthfully, the extra money would help, not to mention less spending on booze."

"Right! Less booze. No ... no booze! More money. More quality time with you. We could even take a vacation together...maybe a second honeymoon."

"Now, don't get carried away. Let's first see how long you can go without drinking."

The last scout meeting was the first weekend in September. Javier was sober and took a deep breath: "Boys. You know you mean a lot to me. But since the incident at Lake Alo, my wife and I have been talking a lot about what to do in the next few years. I've decided that I will no longer be your scoutmaster. I have notified the district, and they will try to find someone to replace me. It's been such a joy for me to have been a part of your lives. My only hope is that because of me you have learned to become good and productive adults. Don't smoke; don't drink; don't hurt anyone; be a Scout for life. I will miss seeing your smiling faces. Come visit me sometime, just to say hello. I will stop drinking. (some muffled laughs) No, really. I mean it. I'm not much for speeches, so that's all I have to say...

"But, before we break tonight, I want to share something with you. You all know how much I admire Charlie Chaplin. Well, a few years ago, I found this poem, which allegedly was written by "The Tramp" himself. If you will indulge me, allow me to share a part of it. I hope you will benefit from it as much as I have."

And with that, Javier unfolded a typed piece of paper and began to read:

As I began to love myself, I found that anguish and emotional suffering are only warning signs that I was living against my own truth.

Today, I know, this is **Authenticity**.

As I began to love myself, I stopped craving for a different life, and I could see that everything that surrounded me was inviting me to grow.

Today I call this **Maturity**.

As I began to love myself, I understood that at any circumstance, I am in the right place at the right time, and everything happens at exactly the right moment. Today I call this **Self-Confidence**.

As I began to love myself, I freed myself of anything that is not good for my health – food, people, things, situations, and everything that drew me down and away from myself...

Today I know it is **Love of Oneself**.

As I began to love myself, I quit trying to always be right, and ever since, I was wrong less of the time.

Today I discovered that is **Modesty**.

As I began to love myself, I refused to go on living in the past and worrying about the future. Now, I only live for the moment, where everything is happening.

Today I live each day, day by day, and I call it **Fulfillment**.

We no longer need to fear arguments, confrontations or any kind of problems with ourselves or others. Even stars collide, and out of their crashing, new worlds are born.

This Today I know **is Life!"**

Javier put down the paper. The room was quiet. Then everyone began to applaud. Still, there was a sense of sadness. We already missed our Scout Leader. It was done!

Months passed. And every week, Javier would say to his wife: "I didn't drink this week. I'm still sober".

His wife would shrug her shoulders and say "So?", as she was not yet convinced that he would actually quit drinking and stay sober ... for good.

And Javier would respond "So? So, sew buttons!"

The same interaction and words were repeated every week. It became their private little joke. Until one day, his wife said "Every week you go without drinking, I'm going to sew a button on the kitchen curtain. I don't think I'll need very many buttons."

The weeks, months, and years passed. Whenever the boys (now men) visited Javier's house, as we often did, just to say "hello", we would see the kitchen curtains covered with buttons, as well as the dining room curtains, the living room curtains, the bedroom and hallway curtains.....

As for us boys: Stick eventually entered the priesthood, after years as an altar boy; Mike and Dan started their own business, "Slim & Slimmer: Accountants"; Roger moved to California with his partner and was working in a place called Silicon Valley; Bruce joined the Marines because he liked their uniforms and TV ads – "Semper Fi, Bruce!"; Twitchy moved to Florida and got involved in politics. He said it made him legitimate. And, lastly, Chico earned a merit badge in Journalism and became an English Literature teacher at a local high school. Me? I spend most of my time writing and making stuff up, while still working hard at letting go of the negative past and learning how to grow-up!

*****

ADDENDUM:

By Timothy Bella and Gina Harkins (Washington Post)
July 2, 2021 at 2:55 p.m. CDT

The Boy Scouts of America reached an $850 million settlement Thursday with tens of thousands of people who say they were sexually abused when they were Scouts over decades and later sued in a case that rocked the historic institution.

The settlement, which came after the organization filed for Chapter 11 bankruptcy last year while facing mounting legal costs over the abuse claims, is one of the largest of its kind in a child sexual abuse case in U.S. history. The lawsuit involved more than 84,000 people who claimed sexual abuse dating as far back as the 1960s.

The agreement — the first legal settlement in a litany of lawsuits against the Boy Scouts — is more than double the group's initial proposal to victims in March. The organization is facing roughly 275 abuse lawsuits and 1,400 potential claims.

(Continued elsewhere)

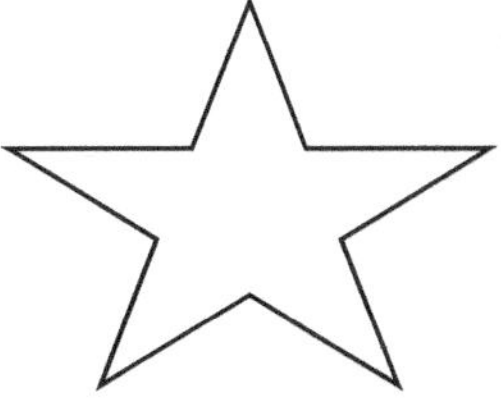

Introduction

It is a wonderful thing to be able to play an instrument – any instrument. One must have the talent to do so, but in addition, one must develop that talent into a skill. Else wise, the talent is never exploited completely.

Most things that have quality are exploited by research (learning) and practice – whether the thing is in sports or the arts or in religion, etc.

Relating to people can also be a talent. Some people are very good at it, others not so. It's easier if you like someone; not so easy if you don't.

Sometimes people do not relate to others who are not like themselves. They may be prejudice, or they may simply have preferences. The color of one's skin or an accent may influence one's likes and dislikes. Ignorance can also work against relating with others.

Our world is filled with different kinds of people. And yet, we can usually find some commonality. There is much "sameness" in the world. Let's develop a talent for finding and exploiting it. Use our God-given talent to better the world.

Piano Lessons

"Music hath charms to soothe the savage beast,

to soften rocks, or bend a knotted oak."

William Congreve

Baseball. How he loved baseball. Carlos was not a very good player. In fact, when the boys in the neighborhood would get together to form teams for a game in the corner vacant lot, he was almost always the last one chosen to play. And what position would he play? He couldn't pitch, catch, or hit very well. And he was already 12 years old.

To the other boys, he seemed smart and fair, so they often chose him to be the umpire -- for home plate and all three bases. That was okay with him; as long as he got to be around the game of baseball. But he rarely got to play, and rarely felt the great satisfaction of a win, a victory. So he joined them as often as he could, whether he played umpire or pinch hitter or substituted for another position. The only set back was equipment. He did not have a glove or a bat or even a ball of his own. So he borrowed. The boys would sometimes sarcastically say to him "Okay, what do you need to borrow today?" It used to bother him; but only for a little while.

What really bothered him was when his mother would walk two blocks down to the vacant lot where they played and call him to come home to eat or do his chores or -- and this was the most embarrassing -- she would yell "Carlos, get out of the sun! It's going to make you real brown. You're going to get dark." It was true. He tanned rather easily. After an hour in the sun, his beige skin would suddenly become bronze and then a dark chocolate brown. And eventually, after many years, it never again lightened to its original color.

She had warned him "If you want to get anywhere in this world, it helps if your skin is lighter." At the time, he could not understand her meaning, and he did not ask her to explain. He just thought aloud "That's dumb! How can lighter skin make me a better baseball player, a better person?"

Then one evening, at dinner, his mother said "I wish you kids would do something more productive than just play baseball." And to my sister "and play with dolls." To the boy she said "You're never going to become a professional baseball player, and you will never make any money playing baseball all the time." He and his sister listened, but pretended not to. She went on "You know that lady down the street? Mary Owen? La India? The Indian woman?"

Carlos and his sister laughed because they had learned in school that Native Americans or American Natives should not be called "Indians." The teacher had explained the whole Christopher Columbus misnomer and all that history stuff. But then again, their mother had only gone as far as the 3rd grade, so maybe she never got far enough in school to learn about Native Americans. They found her use of the word "Indian" to be funny.

"Why are you laughing?" she asked.

The boy said "Mom, they are called Native Americans. Mary is supposed to be a Native American. But, I wonder why, if she is Native American, why does she have a Christian name? Why does she have a name like Mary Owen?"

"I don't know. That's beside the point. Well, you know, she plays the piano. She has one in her living room. I was talking to her a few days ago, and she said that she knows how to teach children to play the piano. So, I want one of you to start taking piano lessons. Mary says she will do it for not too much money. So, which one of you is going to learn to play the piano?"

He did not answer. He just looked down at his plate and started eating faster, expecting her to choose his sister. He thought *not me*; but then his confidence began to wane: *I should just get away from the table before she makes a decision.* But it was too late. She had already made up her mind. She pointed at him. "You, my ball boy son! You will start taking piano lessons every week with Mary, starting next weekend."

The boy's dad entered the kitchen, just having arrived home from work. He sat down at the table and interjected "He should learn to play the drums, like his grandpa."

Protests would be useless. The boy became troubled. "Me? Take piano lessons? Yuck! What about Lucy? She's a girl. She should be the one to take piano lessons." His mother's decision was final. Nevertheless, the next morning, after having slept on the issue, he thought *I guess it won't hurt to give it a shot.*

"But mom, we don't even have a piano" he told her at breakfast.

"I know that. I told Mary that. She said you won't need a piano of your own for quite a while. She said she can teach you on her piano, and that you can practice whenever you want to, using her piano. You know she doesn't work and is home alone almost all the time ... since her sister passed on."

Carlos was only 2 years old when Mary's sister died. He had heard a little about her, but didn't really know her, nor did he know much about Mary.

"But we don't have any music on paper. And even if we did, I don't know how to read music notes."

"You're not going to get out of this that easily. Mary has sheet music and beginner's guides so that you can learn how to read music and play the piano. Music notes are like letters for words. It's like learning a new language. This is something you should *want* to do."

He thought *That is a tricky selling point. Sure! Why wouldn't I want to learn how to play a musical instrument? But a piano?*

"But mom, a piano is too big. What about a guitar or a harmonica?"

"Piano is better. You'll see."

Mary Owen (sometimes referred to as "old lady Owens", with an "s" at the end) lived down the street from where Carlos' family lived. She had been there for as long as he could remember; and was probably there long before he arrived on this good earth. She was not old, compared to other old people in the neighborhood, but she seemed older than she actually was. Almost like she had been through so much strife in her life that she should be really old, and therefore, she looked really old.

She did not always live alone. Mary had a sister, Sarah. For as long as anyone could remember, they had lived together in the small house set far back from the street under two tall elm trees. Their yard was always a mess. They hardly ever cut the grass, and the shrubs and bushes were overgrown and never trimmed. They rarely left their house except to go get groceries. They never went to church nor seemed to mingle with the neighbors, except for the boy's mom. Carlos' mom would often take chocolate candy and vegetables to the sisters; and eventually only to Mary. He never understood why his mom still took food to them. (Later, he would learn that it would be to partially pay for his piano lessons.) The neighbors gossiped that neither sister ever married. They were "old maids". Some kids said that they never got married because they both were too ugly. They were not pretty, that's for sure. Maybe men were just not interested in them; or they were not interested in men. Whatever the reason, they were single and lived alone. They had no children, and apparently no other relatives. They only had each other.

The boy was too young to remember when the younger sister Sarah died. But he was told the story of how the ambulance had come. She was taken from the house on a stretcher or gurney, placed in the ambulance, and with blaring sirens whisked off to the morgue.

People said that Mary did not come out of her house for what seemed like weeks. Everything was very quiet and still for several months. Then one day, the neighbors again heard the familiar sound of the piano inside the house. And Mary was playing again. But now, she was playing her music alone, without her sister's companionship. When Mary finally appeared outside her house, she looked a little older.

That was around ten years ago. Now, the boy found himself walking down the street to Mary Owen's house to begin to learn how to play the piano. It was Saturday, and he would normally be out in the vacant lot waiting to be chosen to play baseball. But here he was, climbing the concrete steps and walking the long walkway to her front door. After a few knocks, the door opened, and there stood Mary. It was the first time he had ever been this close to her and the first time being alone with her in her house. This was very strange to him, and it made him a little anxious. Nevertheless, he pulled himself together and tried to appear calm and relaxed, in spite of feeling unsure and a little fearful.

"You must be Carlos, the boy who wants to learn to play the piano?" she said.

"My mom wants me to learn to play the piano. I don't really care" he said.

"Your mother is a very smart woman" she smiled. "Come in."

Entering the house, he was struck by the "junk" everywhere. There was not a spot in the house not occupied by something...a chair with a stack of magazines on it, a small table cluttered with little objects, the floor with throw rugs, clothes, shoes, newspapers, toys, dolls, even a shovel stood in a corner of the room. All kinds of junk, but, strangely, no TV.

And that's not all. There was a strong odor of something Carlos could not identify. A pungent, unusual smell like something dead cooking on the stove. He did not feel comfortable about this. He was ready to dash out the front door. It was fear; and a "What have I gotten myself into?" kind of feeling.

And then he saw it. There it was. A large high-back, upright piano. Dark wood, like the dark chocolate his mother brought to Mary. He could barely make out the words on the front. "Baldwin" he said softly.

"That's right" Mary said. "Baldwin. It's not one of the best makes, but they've been in business since the 1890s. I only wish I could have afforded a Steinway. They've been in business since the 1850's. Then there's Yamaha. But they're foreign made, so I wouldn't buy one, no matter how good they are... too expensive anyway."

She lifted two booklets from inside the piano bench, then sat on the piano bench and pulled a metal fold-up chair next to her. One book was "Teaching Little Fingers to Play" and the other was D.C. Glover's "Scale Book."

She said "Come sit here. Let's get started."

This was all a little too fast for him. He both wanted to make conversation with her, especially about all the junk in her house; but he also wanted to get out of there as fast as he could. He was being pulled in two opposite directions. Besides, she had very strong breath. It smelled a lot like the rest of the house. *What is that strange smell?*, he thought.

"You know" she said, "Music is the universal language."

"Why? You don't speak it."

"No. But it speaks to anyone who will listen. You perform... you play an instrument and/or you sing. Singing is music too. And no matter in what language you sing, it's pretty much universal because it's just another form of musical expression. In fact, your voice is a musical instrument. When you sing, you're playing your voice."

None of this made much sense to him, but it sure sounded like it made sense. And, he thought, the next time his mom called out to him while he was bathing "What are you doing so long in the tub?", he would answer "Playing my voice!"

Mary began "The first things you will need to learn are the notes -- A through G, some can also be called sharp, and some can also be called flat. Then, once you can identify the notes on the keyboard, you will learn scales. Each scale, called an octave, has 8 notes, not counting sharps and flats, which are usually, but not always, the black keys. I'll explain that later. Once you learn the scales, you can manipulate and arrange them to play music." She pointed to a booklet already on the piano stand, Weybright's "Etudes for Pianists."

He thought *She seems so sure of herself. She seems to think that I can do this. Maybe she is right*. He concluded *maybe I can do this*. And so began the piano lessons.

The days turned to weeks; the weeks into months. He was learning to play the piano. It was possible after all. And yet, during these lessons, in his mind he vicariously played baseball with his friends. But even in his thoughts, the boys often badgered him "Does playing baseball feel the same as playing the keys on a piano?"

*****

Then a curious thing happened. One day, there was a large warehouse fire downtown. Two days after the fire, Carlos' dad was driving home from work, and he passed the partially destroyed warehouse. Outside, near the parking lot, he spotted a much damaged and very old piano, just at the side entrance of the charred building. He stopped and walked over to a man wiping down some office furniture.

"Bad fire, huh?"

"Yeah", the man said. "We're just trying to salvage what we can."

"Is that old piano over there any good?" he asked the man.

"Don't know. Doesn't look like it is. Why you askin'?"

"Well, my son is learning to play piano and we don't have one. If you're gonna throw it away, I'd prefer to take it off your hands. But I can't pay ya for it." The man scratched his head for a second, looked over at the sad-looking piano, and said "Your son, huh? Well, if you can haul it off, it's yours. It's pretty heavy and there's a lot of damage; may not even play."

"No problema" Carlos' dad said. "I'll be right back with a truck."

A few hours later, his dad returned with uncle Bob and Tony from next door. The three of them loaded the old piano onto the truck, brought it to the house, and set it down in the basement, where it was cool and dry. The next day, when the boy got home from school, his dad took him downstairs and showed him the semi-burned, upright piano.

"I bet it sounds real good" the boy's dad said.

Carlos tried to play one of the pieces he had learned from Mary, but it sounded way off key. Not to disappoint his father, he said "Thanks, dad. Now I can practice at home." He had already advanced through Alfred's Basic Piano Library. Things were looking up.

After more than 9 months of piano lessons, Mary announced to the boy that she wanted him to participate in a neighborhood Piano Recital. He had advanced to J.W. Schaum's "Adult at the Piano." She explained that he would be playing with other kids at about the same level of experience; that it was not a competition; but that it was only for the entertainment of people who came to listen to young people play the piano. It would be at a local community center nearby. This proposition made him nervous, but after talking to his mom about it, he agreed.

It was a cool, clear night near the end of February in south Texas. The recital seemed to be a success. The people clapped really hard when he finished his piece. It was a new piece entitled "Wigwam" written by the well known performer, Bob Dylan. It was actually written for guitar, but Mary wanted him to play it, maybe because it had a Native American title, and Carlos had practiced it for quite a while.

He was a little self-conscious that the other performers seemed to play much better than he. But, his parents were, in any case, very proud of him. And he could see that Mary was proud of him too. She had a tear in her eye as he walked passed her after his performance. On the way out of the small auditorium, he overhead a man say of the recital "Well, it's not Chopin, but it'll do." And Carlos thought *Chopin's dead! Huh!* But then he remembered that when he first saw the name Chopin, he had incorrectly but innocently pronounced it 'Choppin'.

Carlos felt that he had finally accomplished something. He had a sense of a win, a victory; something he had never felt after playing baseball. He was glowing with pride.

The week after the recital, the boy went to see Mary. His mom gave him some meatloaf, fruit, and chocolate candy to take to Mary as a gift, because of the recital. Mary was happy to get the gifts but turned down the meatloaf. His mother had forgotten that Mary didn't eat meat.

"I'm vegetarian" she said.

"What's that?" the boy asked. "I thought you were Native American."

She laughed. "I don't eat meat. Vegetarians don't eat animal parts. I only eat fruits and vegetables, and breads." Now, he mistakenly reasoned that the smell in the house was because she only cooked vegetables. Carlos hated the smell of vegetables cooking. "But thank your mom anyway. And, by the way, who taught you to say Native American?"

"In school, the nun, Sister San Juan, said that you are not Indians because this is not India. She said it's more appropriate to call people who lived here long before we did 'Native Americans' or 'American Natives'." Carlos was very proud of this (his) explanation.

"She is right" Mary said. "But there are many tribes and peoples who are Native American. I'm from two tribes. My father was Missouria, which in the Siouan language means 'big canoe people', and my mother was Osage, which is actually one of many Siouan languages. It's too complicated for me to explain, but thanks for recognizing that I'm a Native American."

At that point, he realized that he had established a good enough relationship with Mary that he could finally have a grown-up conversation with her that did not involve piano lessons.

He said "Mary Owen is not a Native American name."

"No. It is not. Mary is my American Christian name. Owen was the name my grandfather took on. He got it from a man he killed in self-defense in 1890."

The boy was taken aback by this revelation. Nevertheless, it did not distract him from wanting to know more about Mary's name.

"But, you're not a Christian. Are you?"

Mary smiled. "I've read about Jesus, and He seems to have been a wonderful and powerful person. There is much I don't understand about Him. Such a good Man to die so horribly! Why did he have to die that way? I wouldn't identify myself by any religion. I just try to lead a good and spiritual life. I hope that's worth something."

Carlos did not quite understand this explanation, but he decided not to pursue it.

"Well, do you have a Native American name?"

"Oh, yes. Weeko. It means 'beautiful girl', which I am not and never was."

"Mary" he said, "What happened to your sister?"

"She died."

"I know that. But I mean what did she die from?"

"Well, I can see you are curious about this, so.... She died of what the doctor called congestive heart failure. He said it was because of the food she ate. I told him that we only eat vegetables, fruits, herbs, and some breads. Well, the doctor just shook his head. Anyway, the good thing was that she did not have to suffer much. She died rather suddenly...very quickly."

"I bet you miss her a lot."

Mary did not respond for a long time. She looked at her piano and softly said "I keep her alive in my heart and in this old piano. I talk to her all the time. One night, I even set the table for two ... old habit. You better get on now. I'm a little tired. Come by next week. We'll talk some more."

"Just one other thing. What is that thing on the shelf? It's neat." He pointed at the object.

"Oh, that is a dream catcher. It was hanging in my bedroom, but I replaced it with a new one, a bigger one I made myself. It's supposed to catch your good dreams so that you can hold on to them. I don't need this one anymore. You can have it if you want." She reached over, caressed it with her hands, and then handed it to him.

"Thanks. I like it. Thanks so much."

"You are welcome. Now you can hold on to your good dreams."

Carlos left feeling very good about himself. He finally had an adult conversation with Mary. He thought *What a genuine person she is! She is the real thing. I have so much to learn from her. Next week, we'll talk some more.* And that night, he looked at the dream catcher thinking *Mary isn't ugly or homely. She is beautiful....and she smells good, like herbs.* He placed the dream catcher under his pillow. He would have many good dreams.

The following week, he arrived eager to talk to Mary. They started their lessons first. After so many months of piano lessons, he now sat alone on the piano bench and played. Mary sat on the metal fold-up chair, directing his performance. When the day's lesson was over, it occurred to him that other than hearing her play the piano from outside on the street, she had never played one of her own pieces for him and for him alone, while he was in her house.

"Mary, before I leave today, would you play something for me? Play one of your favorite pieces. If you don't mind, of course."

She paused for a long time, taking sips from her cup of herbal tea. "Okay. But when I'm done, please leave."

She played beautifully. The loud parts were loud; the soft parts were soft. The flow of the music was mesmerizing. It was a simple song that he had heard before but could not remember its name. As the song was nearing the end, he noticed tears welling up in Mary's eyes. He began to regret asking her to play something, as this seemed to be upsetting her. When she finished with a flourish, there was a long, silent pause.

"That was really nice, Mary. Thank you!"

"It was Sarah's favorite song. It makes me think about... It makes me think deeply."

"I recognize the tune, but I can't remember the name."

"You Are My Sunshine....My Only Sunshine" she said. Then she began to sing a cappella and off key:

"You are my sunshine, my only sunshine. You make me happy when skies are gray. You'll never know, dear, how much I love you. Please don't take my sunshine away."

She closed her eyes and smiled.

Carlos again thanked her, and left quietly, slowly closing the screen door behind him. The birds were tweeting, singing their music, as if they too enjoyed the song that Mary played. He thought about Mary Owen all that week.

The day before he was to meet with her again, he heard the blare of the ambulance and hurried outside. He ran down the street. The ambulance had stopped in front of Mary Owen's house. He waited. And he waited. His heart began to beat fast and heavy. Moments later, he saw the stretcher being rolled out of the house. Although he was only about two years old, and didn't remember when Mary's sister died, he had the same feeling as when he had been told about Sarah...how they had rolled her out on a stretcher or a gurney about 10 years ago.

He overheard a woman standing next to him say to another woman "She was a good person...a good woman, but she wasn't a Christian, and Sarah wasn't really her sister. They were really close, life-long friends, companions... Mary was Indian. They both were, you know."

A little vexed by her comment, he pondered to himself *Indian? She wasn't from India. She was from somewhere around here. Somewhere close to us...somewhere close to me.* And, he also thought, *what does it matter if Sarah was or was not her sister, or her closest friend? Sarah was like a sister. She was Mary's devoted companion until her death.*

He turned and walked slowly back home, contemplating the meaning of loss and death. For the first time in his life, he felt genuine grief. He mused *Maybe she wasn't a Christian. Still, I know that God has welcomed her with open arms. She was, in her own way, Christ-like. Maybe for Mary, heaven is a big room with a grand piano in it.* He hoped so!

As the months passed, his interest in the piano began to wane. His mom and dad were concerned, as they could sense his mourning. He became listless and even abandoned baseball.

He continued to serve as an altar boy at Mass but felt sad that Mary had died and was not Catholic. Nevertheless, he was sure that Mary was in heaven and standing in God's favor.

One morning after Mass, as he removed his cassock, he used it to wipe some tears from his face. He walked home, oblivious to his surroundings. When he got home, he headed downstairs into the basement. And while holding the dream-catcher tightly in his hand, he eyed the marred piano across the room. Alone in the quiet, he spoke aloud:

"What's the use of playing on that old, broken down piano, with keys that are all messed up, and the sound is all wrong? It's just a piece of junk. It needs to be tuned, and we can't afford that. What's the use? Besides, Mary's not around anymore to help me. Why bother?"

Sensing a tear forming, he thought *Mary was old and broken down too, and she was sometimes off key. She was kinda like this old piano. She was not burned in a fire, but she had been burned and scarred when Sarah died. She had been through a lot. Mary was my sunshine for a while.*

Carlos walked out of the basement room and never returned to play the piano again. And he never got any better at baseball either!

As we navigate through life, we cognitively and emotionally move from family, friends, and school, to family, friends and work. But we never forget school.

Elementary school can be a blur. But high school – in the 50s and 60s grades 9-12 -- can be particularly memorable. We can actually be away from home ... on our own, conditionally.

Teachers replaced parents and other adult family members. Who were they to us? Role models, disciplinarians, parent substitutes? They were (are) all that and more. They were strangers to us, at first. Yet they became parts of our psyche. Through them we acquired perspective and attitude. We grew in so many ways; and yet they remained constant – in spite of changes in their lives. They were vulnerable leaders. They imparted more than book knowledge.

Teachers Extraordinaire

"What nobler employment, or more valuable to the state, than that of the man [woman] who instructs the rising generation?"

Cicero

For most people who finished 12 years of school, there is at least one or two teachers who stand out in their memory; someone who made a special impression on them. For me, in my senior year, there were two such teachers, who today, 50+ years later, I still remember fondly.

Ms. Lila T. Vandenberg was a special teacher. She taught senior-level American and World Literature. It was because of her, that I developed an appreciation of literature. Having a teenage crush on her also helped to stir my interest in books and all printed matter.

She was soft-spoken, yet, as I surmised, did everything by the book. She taught literature because it was obvious that she loved literature and loved helping her students come to appreciate its value. "Reading also helps us to write and communicate better", she would say.

The first day of class, she gave us a list of books to read outside of class, and we were to write a 500-700 word summary of the book. We were required to read one book a week. I wanted to impress her, so I read the first book that night, and also wrote a 600-word summary. The next day before class began, I walked up to her.

"Ms. Vandenberg, I read the *Red Badge of Courage* last night and also wrote my summary. Can I hand it in today?" She seemed a little taken back, but also pleased.

"Why, yes, Leonard. That will be fine. I look forward to reading your summary."

"And I can read another book tonight and write a summary. In fact, I can read a book every night and write a summary."

"Wow, my goodness! That's very ambitious of you. But if that's what you want to do, well then I'll be more than happy to accept your summaries. But, I hope you're not just reading the abridged versions or the Cliff Notes".

"Oh, no, Ms. Vandenberg! I can get the books from the library and read the entire original version. I'll even buy a book if I have to."

"Well, okay. We'll talk more about this later, because it's time for class now."

She was single, about 35 years old, thin, with big brown, bovine eyes. None of us knew anything about her background, where she came from or if she was born here. Her name was intriguing because nobody I knew had a last name like hers. It almost sounded like royalty to me. I thought *Maybe she's a princess, or maiden or damsel.* In any case, it was easy to like her, and I wanted to impress her. And, so I did.

I did not know what teachers did when they were not at school. The only other time they were seen was at PTA meetings and at course grade and performance reviews, usually with a parent. I wanted to know more about Ms. Vandenberg - where she lived, what she did outside of school, more about her personal life.

One day, I did not immediately go home after school. I waited in the parking lot where I had a clear view of the Staff Parking. It was around 5:30 PM that I spotted Ms. Vandenberg walking to her car, carrying a shoulder bag and a large brief case. It was the first time I saw the car she drove – an old 1956 yellow Ford. It didn't seem to match her personality. I followed her in my car as she drove home. I kept my distance so as not to be detected.

She came to a quaint neighborhood about 10 miles from school. She parked in her driveway and went inside. I felt a little guilty spying on her, but I did not feel that I was doing anything wrong. I just wanted to get to know her better. I waited, but was not sure why or for how long I should stay. It wasn't long when the front door opened, and she escorted an old man with a cane to her car. She opened the passenger door for him, and he got in. She then sat in the driver's seat and drove off.

Again, I followed at a distance, until she arrived at a strip mall. There, she escorted the old man into a restaurant. I assumed it might be her father. He was too old to be her husband. Then I drove home.

After this incident and others that followed, I came to understand that Ms. Vandenberg was caring for her aging father, but her mom was not in the picture. I thought *What a kind and caring daughter she is*! I would keep this little secret to myself. I would never tell her that I had been spying on her.

Near the end of the first semester, feeling a little bolder, and maybe a little foolish, I approached her after class.

"Lila! May I call you Lila, Ms. Vandenberg?"

"I don't think that's a good idea, Leonard. I am your teacher and you are my student. Don't you think that would be disrespectful?"

She was right, of course. But I felt rejected. I felt betrayed. I thought we had developed a close relationship due to all the reading I had done and summaries I had submitted to her on a daily basis. She gave me an A in almost all my summaries. To me, this was a sign that she reciprocated my affections. I was neglecting my other courses due to my devotion to her and the assignments. Couldn't she see that I was in love with her, and that I would do anything for her?

Before Winter Break, she told me "Leonard, you're a fine young man, and someday, maybe you will have a wife, someone closer to your age; someone you will have more in common with."

"You can call me Lenny. You and I...we have a love of literature in common. Don't we?"

"Yes, Lenny, but there is more to life than that. I want you to continue to read as much as you can. But, I want you to see me as your teacher and nothing more. Someday, maybe you'll understand that one's position and status in life are important. We don't always get what we want, Leonard. We sometimes have to accept what is, and be as satisfied as we can with that."

Her words lost their meaning. She was speaking, but I stopped listening. How could she do this to me? Didn't she read "Lady Chatterley's Lover"? But, by now, I was sure that she was aware of my feelings for her.

I would have to endure this spurning for the remainder of my senior year. But this did not mitigate my growing passion for reading almost anything I could get my hands on. She introduced me to Salinger and Virginia Wolfe; Harper Lee and Ray Bradbury; Jane Austen and Nathaniel Hawthorne; Joseph Conrad and Mark Twain; Herman Melville and Charles Dickens; Ann Frank and the Brontes; Cervantes and Gide; Stein and Steinbeck; Faulkner and Ferber. The list was as long as a country road. Ralph Ellison and James Baldwin; Franz Kafka and J.R. Tolkien; poets such as Walt Whitman and e.e. cummings. One valuable gift I acquired from Ms. Vandenberg was a love of literature. And for that, I am forever grateful.

The first day of the second semester, Ms. Vandenberg announced to the class that her father had passed away over the Christmas Holiday. She said that she had been caring for him over the past 10 years. She said she wanted to tell us this because "death is such an important theme in literature. It is the one constant that applies to all living things."

"When someone dies" she said, "it's not important what matters to them. That is out of our hands. We have no say in what happens to them after their death. We can only guess or assume. What is important is what happens to us as survivors. If you loved the one who died, then you will miss them terribly. You will feel sad, and feel that a piece of you is now missing. So what you do after someone you loved dies is very important. Understand that funerals, burial arrangements, cremations and memorial services are for the living, and not for the dead. The deceased have no use for what we do after they die. I had my father cremated, because that was his wish. His cremains are in an urn that I keep in the hallway of my house. That is for me; not for him. I am at peace now, because I believe that he is at peace."

The students were silent, but not without sadness and empathy. The next day, I bought a sympathy card, and almost all the students in the class signed it. I gave it to Ms. Vandenberg, and she was very thankful. I felt at peace, too.

Later in the second semester, it was rumored that Ms. Vandenberg was engaged to be married. I was crushed, at first.

In class, a student asked "Is it true you're gonna get married, Ms. Vandenberg?"

Some students giggled, and I looked around the room feeling somewhat embarrassed.

"As a matter of fact, students, I am engaged to be married this summer. I am very happy and excited about this, and I hope you feel the same for me."

The students all responded "yes, yes...sure". Everyone, except me. I remained stoic and expressionless. It did not go unnoticed by Ms. Vandenberg. She smiled at me.

After class, she stopped me: "Lenny, be happy for me. I'm happy."

I turned and walked out of the room.

It took me several months to begin to forgive her. Prom was coming up, so I was thinking about who I should ask to accompany me. I eventually decided on Olga. She was pretty, and she was charming. I always found her pleasant and appealing. When I popped the question to her, she responded very positively: "I thought you'd never ask. I already turned down two other guys. Of course I'll go to the prom with you."

Prom night was wonderful. Olga and I had the best time. We talked on the phone for hours after that. I began to realize we had a lot in common and would be attending the same college. We shared a lot of our feelings. I even told her how I once felt about Ms. Vandenberg. She thought that was "sweet". I did not tell her about the spying.

Things took a turn for me that summer. I was not invited to Ms. Vandenberg's wedding, which I heard was really fabulous. But I could understand. If she invited one student, she'd have to invite everybody. Besides, it was a private affair, with a small gathering of their families and close friends. After the wedding, the newlyweds moved out of state to start a new life together. And that was okay by me. My focus had turned from Ms. Vandenberg to Olga.

Yet, in reality, I have never stopped feeling strongly about my senior literature teacher. She will always remain close to my heart and a prominent figure in my memory. She introduced me to the world of literature, the meaning and importance of words; the written experiences of men and women from around the world, historically and currently. How wonderful is that?

I still love to read, and Ms. Vandenberg would be proud of me. I often wonder if she ever thinks about me. Maybe my high school crush was more than a juvenile heartthrob. Maybe she was my first true love. Innocence and naiveté are two aspects of first love. And there's no sin in that. I will never forget her or how she made me feel. She made me feel valued.

I can appreciate why Mexicans, and probably most other Hispanics, give their daughters feminized male names. Such was the case with Mrs. (Sra.) Rafaela Vega. Did her parents want a son, whom they had planned to name Rafael, but got a daughter instead? And so they named her Rafaela? It's really pretty easy to feminize a name. One merely adds the letter "a" to the end of the male name. *Voila, Rafaela!* Likewise, in English, there's Eric and Erica!

Rafaela Vega was my Spanish teacher. Some of the boys made fun of her initials R.V. We could sometimes be cruel at that age. I spoke Spanish at home sometimes, but almost exclusively to my grandparents. English was, and is, my dominant and primary language. My Spanish was more Spanglish than anything. So I decided to take two years of H.S. Spanish to learn to speak and to write that Romantic language correctly.

Mrs. Vega was a short stocky woman of about 50. Some would call her frumpy or matronly. She had thick auburn hair and wore a lot of lipstick and eye shadow. She was married to a man who neighbors said was “lazy and doesn’t want to work”.

The couple had three children, the youngest one, a 17 year old, lived at home and attended the same school. He did not take Spanish, but he would spend a lot of time with Mrs. Vega when she was not in class. He was smart, but shy. He also had a drinking problem. No, not alcoholism. Water. It was a condition I learned years later that is called Hyponatremia. At that time, there was no established treatment for this disorder. It was so serious a problem to the boy, I heard, that one day, he took the outside water hose and put it into his mouth and turned on the water. He drank so much water, so fast, that he passed out on the lawn. Fortunately, his sister found him and rushed him to the E.R., where he was pumped and treated. He survived, but I guess it was a scary situation for everybody. It was a warning sign. His water intake had to be perpetually monitored. His medical condition was the cause of much worry for Mrs. Vega.

Sra. Vega always seemed "tired", "fatigued". It was rumored that she was the only one in the household who was working full time. Her husband did not work, except for odd jobs, when he felt like it. Her teenage son occasionally did yard work in the neighborhood too, but she needed to check on him frequently. On weekends, Mrs. Vega would do laundry for a few middle- to upper-class families. I once overheard her tell another teacher "A woman's work is never done." I found that interesting.

In Spanish classes, I did not just learn to speak, write, improve spelling and grammar, and communicate better, but there were other things that made the courses more interesting. There were cultural issues that we discussed, and we reviewed the various Hispanic dialects based on countries: Mexican, Cuban, Puerto Rican, Dominican, the Central American and the South American cultures and dialects. Sra. Vega explained that the same applied to English. We speak American English, she said, which is different from British or the King's English, which is also different from the English spoken in Australia, New Zealand, and even in Ireland, Scotland, and Wales. This was all a little overwhelming to me. And there was more.

"Even here in America" she explained, "There are many identifiable dialects or 'accents' depending on where you were raised. Southerners have a form of speaking that is different from the way people in the New England area speak. You can certainly tell the difference between a New Yorker and a Bostonian and an Alabamian. The northern mid-west speech sounds different from the lower mid-west. And people in Louisiana have a distinct accent. But it all works out. We all understand each other in the end. That's the beauty of language."

"In America", she explained, "the diversity in the English language reflects the diversity of its people. Heterogeneity is what makes America so complex, yet fascinating and dynamic. The same can be said of Spanish, with its diversity of cultures and dialects.

"Hispanic, Latino and Spanish are not homogeneous, but heterogeneous concepts. And yet, the issues are not about differences, but rather about respect and acceptance. Not to have respect for our differences, as well as for our commonalities, would be like not accepting a rainbow because of its different colors. America is one great and wonderful mosaic."

Then there was the matter of the history of Spanish in America. Mrs. Vega provided handouts on this topic. She explained that the first English-speaking colony in America was at what is now Jamestown, Virginia around 1607. It was named after King James I, who granted the charter a year earlier in 1606. The colony consisted of both men and women - families. The settlement originally numbered about 214 people, but within two years, only 60 had survived. This was the result of disease and battles with the native peoples, primarily the Algonquians.

Many more families arrived over the next ten years. The first organized government assembly for these newcomers did not convene until 1619. And, in 1620, the Mayflower, with 102 passengers, docked at what is now Provincetown, Cape Cod, Mass. And in November of 1621, the Pilgrims celebrated their first harvest. It became known as *Thanksgiving*.

There was a significant contrast to the English-speaking immigrants (settlers) and their Spanish-speaking counterparts: In time-lines, numbers, genders, goals, and processes.

Much earlier, Columbus and the Spanish crews arrived in the Caribbean in August of 1492, on three ships and an undetermined number of men, no women. By October 1492, 39 men had established colonies in the Bahamas, Cuba, and Hispaniola. Columbus carried treasures along with indigenous natives back to Spain, and then returned to the colonies in 1493 with 17 small ships and 1,500 men. In contrast to the English-speaking settlers, few, if any, families made the "exploratory" voyages. Such adventures were reserved for men!

Spanish became the official language; and, it was imposed on the native peoples, as was Catholicism. The population grew exponentially due to the blending of the Spaniards and the native women. Having crossed the ocean without female companionship, the indigenous women became the mates to the Spaniards.

By 1513, Ponce de Leon had begun to establish colonies in Florida. And in 1565, he and his men founded St. Augustine, Florida, the oldest continuously occupied European city in the United States. It is estimated that between 1492 and 1832, nearly two million Spaniards settled in the Americas.

"Today, after English, Spanish is the most common language in the U.S." continued Mrs. Vega. "Spanish and English are the official languages of New Mexico and Puerto Rico. For many years, up to the Louisiana Purchase, Spanish was the primary language in most states west of the Mississippi River. With the influx of more Spanish speakers into America, Spanish has become the second most commonly spoken language in almost every U.S. state. In fact, many American states, cities, regions, islands, streets and roads have Spanish proper names. In a sense, Spanish *is* an American language."

Mrs. Vega wanted us to know this because it added to the importance of learning to speak and write Spanish. She reinforced its value in our society and in the beautifully woven tapestry that is America.

It was around March of my senior year that a substitute teacher walked into the classroom. He said that Mrs. Vega would not be available to teach the class. Her hiatus would last for several weeks. He explained that it was a family matter, and that he was not authorized to talk about it. He would cover for her until her return.

Classes with Mr. Collins lasted over two weeks. Within that time, we learned that Mrs. Vega's son had drowned in the bathtub of their home. Her husband found him, face down. Such a tragedy! We all felt terrible and heartbroken for her. Similar to what we did for Ms. Vandenberg, a few of us bought her an oversized sympathy card in Spanish, and everyone signed it. We made sure it had a religious theme. There was nothing else we could do.

Mrs. Vega returned to class in early April. She seemed older and somewhat spent. How painful it must have been for her to have lost a child, her youngest. How very sad for everyone!

Nevertheless, she smiled and told us she was happy to be back in the classroom with us. "Let me get this out of the way", she said. She was very open and told us what had happened. She talked about her son in a most loving way. About the incident, she said that it was God's will. "My son is at peace, now. When he was much younger, he was an altar boy at our church. He loved serving at Mass because it made him feel important and needed. He was so young and innocent. I still have his cassock. Caring for him the 17 years that he lived was my privilege.

"Students, when an older person -- a grandparent or any older loved one -- dies, we lose a part of the past. When we lose a spouse, a sibling, or a friend – a contemporary, a peer -- we lose a part of the present. But when a child, a daughter, a son, or any young person dies, we lose a part of the future. My family and I have lost a big part of our future."

In the aftermath of this tragedy, we all saw Mrs. Vega in a different light. She was a human being, compassionate and dedicated to her craft. She was a loving mother and wife. Her strength and fortitude were undeniable. The word *courage* came to my mind as she remained focused on sticking to the curriculum, "staying the course", ever the professional and maternal teacher. That was the Sra. Vega I came to know and admire.

To our surprise, she decided to take some time off at the end of this semester. She announced that this would be her last year of teaching "for a while." It may have been a sabbatical from school, but not from teaching. I later learned that she started doing some tutoring with the children of the families she did laundry for. That summer I also learned that her husband had started a full-time job and that he had become her strongest supporter, in every way. The death of their son brought them closer together. Their two older children also spent more time involved in family matters. Their family unit was reinforced, strengthened.

Strange how death can change personal and familial relationships! However, the nature of that change seems to be up to us. That two people had died during my last semester in high school was a coming of age experience I did not expect. I did not even know these two individuals, and yet I was moved by the response of the two women I did know.

Again, the theme of death and dying became clearer to me. Ms. Vandenberg was right. What's important is what happens to survivors after the loss of a loved one. Mrs. Vega not only taught me Spanish. She and Ms. Vandenberg taught me life lessons about death.

These were two very different women who shared a love of teaching and a commitment to those they taught. They were not only teachers, they were caregivers; surrogates, albeit temporary, and part-time parents. They did more for others than for themselves. Two very different women, who were very much alike in so many ways, sharing the same values and dedication. And yet, in the flow of life, each went her own way, setting her own path.

I recall Ms. Vandenberg once telling us "Your first teacher is your heart. It teaches you to care. It makes everything else you learn make sense."

After high school, I went on to college and came to know and admire many professors and lecturers. They were very smart and were experts in their fields. I truly respected them. But my two high school teachers remain constants in my life.

My heart has taught me this: It taught me to never forget the gifts Ms. Vandenberg and Mrs. Vega gave to me -- the gift of understanding as well as the value of learning.

Ref.: historymania.com/American_history/Spanish_in_the_United_states

Ref.: preservationvirginia.org/rediscovery/

Introduction

Near the end of the Vietnam War (November 1955 – April, 1975), I was in college (1966 – 1970). I did not serve in the military and was given a college deferment. But some of my high school friends and relatives did serve. A few never returned.

Most Americans were deeply affected by this conflict. Many minority boys/men were drafted; and many in my little barrio wore the uniform(s). After more than 50 years, I still think of them. I wonder what would have become of their lives; what they might be doing today.

This story is about a painful loss as a result of that war. And yet, it is a story of inspiration and endurance. This man writes about his beloved cousin, Christina.

Christina

"The Heart is a Lonely Hunter"
-- Carson McCullers

My cousin Christina was pretty when she was young: still is. She was the youngest of three girls whose father was German American and her mother, my aunt, was Mexican American. Christina was short and thin, fair-skinned, with hazel eyes and a killer smile. My aunt would often comment, "She's going to break a lot of hearts." True enough.

We went to school together from elementary through high school, until I graduated from 12th grade. There were always boys following her, wanting to be around her, wanting to be with her. She liked the attention in some ways. But in other ways, she was basically shy, and was a little embarrassed by all this admiration; shy, but not quiet with me or with family members and close friends. We hung out a lot and shared our feelings and thoughts.

The boys knew that I was her cousin; hence, I was no threat to them. They would often come to me and ask me to give her "messages". Or they would ask me questions like "Do you think Christina likes me?" It was all really very innocent, for the most part.

By what I observed, Christina was smart. She earned good grades, but she studied a lot. She was popular with the other girls in school, too. It may be that she got a lot of good advice from her two older sisters, who were also attractive and smart in school.

My aunt emphasized education. And Christina was not a party girl. With the exception of birthdays and her Quinceanera, she did not partake in parties and festivities outside the immediate family. Her two older sisters, on the other hand, never turned down an invitation for potential fun. They dated ... a lot. I would describe them as “boy-crazy.”

Christina turned down most invitations to date. She would tell me that the boy was too skinny, or too fat, or too dumb, or smelled funny or he just wanted to "you know what!” She admitted to me that she was “on the hunt” for the right guy, maybe someone like her dad, who had divorced her mother and moved out of state. She would be patient and wait for the right guy to come along, for as long as it took.

“I just want to make sure he is ‘the one’. I’m sure I’ll know him when I meet him.”

It was during her freshman year, that Christina's mother and father decided to divorce. I did not know, nor did I want to know, all of the details. When he moved out of town, he left my aunt to care for the three girls. I really liked him and could not understand why they saw it necessary to separate and go their own ways. Christina was very close to her dad, and she was deeply upset by the divorce and her dad's departure.

Several months later, she said "My daddy sent me and my sisters a letter." She read the letter to me: "My Dear Beautiful Daughters, I love you all very, very much, and I will miss you until the next time I am with you. You will always be in my heart and on my mind. I am sorry about the divorce and any pain it may have caused the three of you, my sweethearts. Take good care of your mother. She is a wonderful woman, and she was an understanding and caring wife to me. I look forward to the day that I am with you again. In the meantime, I will send some money on a regular basis to help your mother with expenses. With all my love, hugs, and kisses. Always ... Dad."

Christina and her sisters never saw their dad again, and no money ever came.

Nearly three years later, Christina's oldest sister was expecting a baby. She had not married, but everyone knew who the father was, because she had been dating the same boy for over a year. The boy had already graduated from High School.

Christina's mom was devastated for two reasons. First of all, her oldest daughter was not married, and she was just about to graduate from High School. She was already beginning to show the signs of pregnancy. The family decided that she and the boy would have to get married, immediately. The boy and his family concurred. The oldest sister and the boy reluctantly agreed. Secondly, and even more disturbing, my aunt became pregnant at about the same time as her oldest daughter. For whatever reason, this co-pregnancy or dual-pregnancies, was just about the worst thing that could happen to my aunt. She refused to be seen in public with her oldest daughter. Mother and daughter each obviously expecting a child at the same time! It was shameful and embarrassing to her. My aunt had not remarried, but she had been dating. And now, by her standards, she and her oldest daughter were paying the price.

Christina, on the other hand, was accepting and even agreeable to the entire situation. She was soon to have a niece or nephew, as well as a new, baby sister or baby brother. As it turned out, she got a baby niece from her sister and a baby brother from her mother, both born within a month of each other. She was happy with her new roles as both aunt and older sister. We were all growing up much too fast.

About the time that both babies were born, Christina started seriously dating a young man she had met after church services one Sunday. Everyone was curious and yet delighted that someone finally met her approval. His name was Christopher...Chris. He was about a year or two older than Christina. He was thin, not too tall, friendly and vivacious. Like me, he was dark-skinned, and he was considered very handsome by everyone who knew him. Some of the descriptions were “cute”, “a real cutie”, “a hunk”, “gorgeous”, and “eye candy”. And, best of all, he had a job. Like Christina's oldest sister, he had already graduated from High School and had been working for a stationary company for over two years. He came from a family that was well liked and respected in the community... a hard working Christian family.

“Really?” I said sarcastically. “Chris and Christina? Really? What are the odds?”

“I know”, Christina laughed. “I guess it was just meant to be. Fate!”

A year later, Christina confided in me "I think he's the one!" I was happy for the both of them. I told her "Be careful. Remember what happened to your sister.” "Oh", she said. "You don't have to worry about that. I'm not going to do anything until...that is, unless we get married and not before." And then she added "You're the one who'd better be careful. That Loretta is hot to trot. Yeah, she sure has the hots for you, cuz!" She was referring to the girl I was dating, and I too knew better than to go "too far" with her. Besides, my interests were elsewhere, and not with Loretta and her kind!

"Right!" I said. "Do you think he wants to marry you?"

"I'm pretty sure he does, but we're both too young. Don't you think?"

"Yes I do. Has he tried to get into your pants yet?"

"No, silly! You've seen us kiss and hold hands and go out and everything.

“That's all that goes on. We have a lot of things in common. We both want to wait until it’s the right time."

"Yeah. I bet you do." I joked.

After graduating from High School, I saw very little of my cousin Christina and Chris. I went off to college out of state. She stayed home and got a job in a candy factory, while at the same time helped care for her baby niece and baby brother. She also continued to see, on a daily basis, what seemed to me to be the love of her life.

She and Chris were very patient, and some would say prudent. They wanted to wait until they were absolutely certain that they were meant for each other before they would tie the knot. I was not surprised at Christina's self-discipline. I knew she wanted to marry Chris. I knew she wanted this relationship to be done right, with honor, and respectfully. I knew she would wait, and that he would wait for her. And so they waited. And, I anxiously waited, too.

"December 01, 1968. Greetings:" So the letter began. Chris received his Draft Notice from SSS when he was 19. Nevertheless, he was surprised. When a young man reached draft age, he knew that it was only a matter of time before the notification would arrive.

We all had been following the Viet Nam War and the devastation it was causing here at home, as well as abroad. Regardless of one's perspective of the war, young men were being drafted and were needed in order to keep the war effort strong. The government was determined that the U.S.A. would win its battle against the North Vietnamese Communists. When a young man was drafted, he either had to go in for induction or seek a legitimate deferment; or illegally avoid the draft entirely. Some men voluntarily enlisted in one of the armed forces. Even members of the National Guard were eligible for active duty overseas. Of course, one could get an automatic deferment if he failed the physical exam or was found not to be of sound mind.

I had received my notice months later. I was eventually granted a College Deferment; with an open recall should the situation in Vietnam worsen. Chris was strong, healthy, and very much of sound mind. He would have been successful in any branch of service, or in any profession for that matter. He went for his physical and was inducted as a draftee, which meant that he had a pretty good chance of being sent into combat in Southeast Asia.

I was with the inseparable couple when the two of them discussed their challenging situation.

“I’m okay with this”, he told Christina. "I'll serve my two or three years and then come back home. My boss says my job will be here for me when I get back."

"I'm scared", she said.

"Don't be. I want to marry you. I want to marry you now...before I leave."

For Christina, this would be one of the most difficult moments in her life and one of the most difficult replies for her to say to Chris.

"No, Chris. I want to wait until you come back home. I love you, and I will wait for you to come back. I promise I'll wait, and when you get back we'll have a big, traditional Mexican wedding! And I’ll wear all white."

He could not look at her face. He looked down at his dusty shoes. She held him, embraced him, squeezed him, and kissed him.

"Okay", he said. "It's not what I had planned, but I guess if you say you'll still be here for me, then that's the way it's goin' to be. You won't date anyone else? It's going to be hard. When I get back, I want us to have a kid right away."

"Of course we will, silly. That's what I want, too. But it definitely won't be right away. I won’t date anybody else. Cross my fingers! And I definitely won't even look at another guy! Double cross my fingers! Promise!"

It was a difficult situation for both of them. I knew, or at least I was fairly certain, that Christina was still a virgin, and she assured me that Chris was too. I had no reason not to believe her. Still, the decision not to marry and to wait until Chris returned from military duty was a risky one. The decision seemed to be practical, mature, and moral. Who could argue that this beautiful young couple had not made the right decision? I was proud of her and of Chris. They both showed a lot of restraint and great fortitude.

I met up with Christina the following summer, while home between semesters. It was the occasion of our annual summer family reunion. I asked her about Chris. She seemed eager to talk about him. She showed me some of his letters and even read parts of them to me. She also carried a picture of Chris in his uniform which, with great pride, she held up close to my face.

"Isn't he the most handsome of handsome?" I agreed. She was so happy that he was safe and thinking of her every day. For her part, she was counting the days until his return. She was already putting together some of the preliminary wedding plans.

"So how's *your* love life, Cuz?" she grinned and swayed.

"Don't ask! And stop being so coy!" I said.

“If you had someone, we could all get married on the same day.” We laughed.

At the end of Summer I returned to college and continued to pursue my degree program. My mind was focused only on school work. I didn't have time for a love life. I told myself "All school and no play....will pay off on graduation day." I'm an eternal optimist.

When the fall semester ended in December, I took a few days for myself. I stuck around the dorm, read the Bible, studied maps, and peacefully listened to my favorite classical composers: Bach, Beethoven, and

Brahms. By the 23rd of December, I was ready to go home for the Christmas Holiday.

It was cold in the city. There was a light snow in north Texas, which I had hoped for, because the snow added to the spirit of the Yuletide season. My parents' house was warm and cheerful. The aroma of freshly steamed tamales, coffee, and baked banana-nut bread filled our humble home. The tree was sparkling and was lit with colorful lights. I drank eggnog, seasoned with bourbon, and there was Christmas music in the background. These times still remain happy, heartfelt memories.

Our conversation turned to the family, and I asked about Christina.

"Oh, I told you about her fiancé didn't I?" my mom asked.

"No..."

"Oh, good Lord! I'm so sorry, *mijo*. He was killed in Viet Nam."

At that moment, if I could have said something, I would have gasped "What?" Instead, my throat tightened, and no words came out of my dry mouth. As the shock slowly subsided, my thoughts turned to Christina. *She must feel completely lost.* I needed to go see her, right away.

My mother was apologetic, but it was just as much my fault because I had been remiss in keeping in contact with the family. And yet, no one was at fault. Getting the news, especially bad news, later than sooner, seemed irrelevant at that point.

I called Christina, and my aunt answered the phone. I told her I wanted to come by. She asked me to wait and come by the next day. And so, I did.

My aunt's house was quiet and still. The air was still. There was little in the atmosphere of her house to suggest that it was Christmas. Christina was congenial, as I offered my condolences. On the surface, she seemed to be handling it well. But of course, I knew that she was suffering inside. I could only imagine her pain. We made small talk and then turned our attention, as if to distract ourselves, to the two smaller kids, her little brother and niece. Two hours later, I left their house feeling less than helpful. What could I do? What could I say?

This would be my last direct contact with Christina for several years. I wondered how long it would take her to start the "hunt" again for Mr. Right; or if she would or could ever give her heart to another.

After college, I landed a job teaching High School physics out of state. I decided to focus on my career and eventually get into a Doctoral Degree program, and move up to teaching at the college level. I was accepted into a graduate program at a major university. I continued to take courses there, meeting the requirements for an advanced degree, while working part-time. This took longer than I had anticipated. I had always worked part-time while going to school, so this was not new territory for me. Work was a nice break from school, and school was a nice break from work.

Eventually, I completed the program and earned a Ph.D. I had applied for several teaching positions and was fortunate to land one in yet another state. This of course meant relocating, again. Flexibility is a necessity when trying to establish one's career early on.

There were occasional visits home, but I never seemed to find time or need to reconnect with Christina, her sisters, or my aunt. Deep down, I think I avoided them because I felt that there was really nothing I could do to make their lives better. Wrongly, I felt that I had outgrown them. I saw their lives static and uneventful. I was drifting away from them and from a lot of the people I had been close to when I was growing up. I even stopped going home for the annual family reunions. I no longer felt that I had much in common with "the old gang". I regret those temporary seasons of pride and arrogance -- collateral damage resulting from “independence” and higher education.

In July of 1988, I had decided to attend a conference in Washington, D.C. I had met someone several years earlier, so my partner and I traveled to D.C. together and checked into a modest hotel we had booked earlier. I had called my parents and told them about the conference, but I hadn't told them where we would be staying.

Our first night at the hotel, I called them to let them know the name of the hotel. I had learned that some things never change, and one of those things was keeping communication channels open, at least by phone, between Mom and me. Although, I was often not very good at it. I would not make the same mistake I made when Chris died. Nowadays, little time would lapse between my calls home.

On the phone Mom said, "Well you guys enjoy yourselves. And if you have time, be sure to take a tour of the White House and the Capital and all those big monuments they have up there. And, take a lot of pictures!"

"Okay, Mom. We plan to, right after the conference closes. Bye now!"

The conference was informative, and we met a lot of nice people. I made some connections and contacts with other Physics teachers, who still remain friends and colleagues of mine. They encouraged me to apply for a better paying position and gave me “contacts.”

The day before the conference ended, I had a message waiting for me at the front desk of the hotel. It was from Christina, asking me to call her. She left a number. That evening, after dinner, I called.

"Your mom told us you were in Washington, D.C. Wow! That must be awesome." She sounded like the sweet teenage girl I knew years earlier.

Pleased to hear her voice, I replied "Gosh, it's been so long since we've talked. So good to hear from you! And, yes, D. C. is beautiful. Big. But very hot and humid. You should come see it someday."

"Well, you know me. I never go anywhere... with the family and all, you know." Christina had married several years after Chris' death. She now had two kids of her own. I did not know and had never met her husband or her children. I had heard that she and her family were doing "okay". I heard that her husband was a “good” man, but the family secretly maintained “but he's no substitute for Chris.”

Wanting to make her feel good, I said "I can understand. Family can be a lot of work and a lot of responsibility I don't have to worry about that, at least not for now. Who knows? Maybe someday! Anyway, how have you been, sweetie?"

"I've been good...very good. But I wanted to call and talk to you for a specific reason."

"Sure! Okay! What is it?"

"Well, I may never get to Washington, at least not any time soon. So, I was wondering if you would do me a big favor. Only if you can, and if you have time. I hate to ask."

"No, no. Not to worry. All I can do is say yes or no or whatever. What is it?"

"Well, Chris... you remember... Chris."

Her voice took a different tone, more somber. My heart started to beat stronger. I felt flushed. "Yes. Of course I do."

"Chris's name should be on the wall of the Vietnam Veterans Memorial. I've heard that people can get tracings of the names. Do you think you can get me some kind of rubbing or tracing of his name? I mean, I know it's a lot to ask...."

"No, no. It's not a problem. I'll see what I can do. Don't worry. That shouldn't be a problem. We were planning on going there anyway."

"Well, if you can. And, also if you can, would you mail it to me. I'll give you my new home address."

"Sure, not a problem. But first let me make sure I'm allowed to do this. Okay?"

"Okay...Thanks so much. You don't know how much this means to me."

Actually, I did. We had not planned on going to the Viet Nam Veterans Memorial, but I understood how much this meant to Christina. We would go to the Wall!

After Chris' body was flown home, funeral services soon followed. His family had given Christina the American flag provided by the army, along with his ID (dog tags) at the memorial service. But she wanted to see more of his name...or better, perhaps symbolically, she wanted *to have his name*...always.

The Vietnam Veterans Memorial was started in 1982, with some controversy surrounding Maya Lin, the young architect who designed it. And it was officially dedicated in November of 1984. Since then, thousands have visited The Wall, or The Wall That Heals, as it is sometimes called, to honor those who served in that horrific war. There are 58,272 names on the panels, including those recently added. Names are still being added today. Whether one was in favor of or opposed to the war, most Americans supported the men and women who served. And for those who perished, their deaths were not in vain. Fortunately, there was (is) a system that helps survivors of the fallen with "name rubbings".

Because of Christina, I felt it my obligation, my duty, and an honor to go to the Wall and fulfill her request.

The day after the conference ended, my partner and I ventured out to tour the city; including paying a visit to The Wall...It was our first stop.

We parked our rented car several blocks away. The crowds were still large, with long lines of people waiting to pass through. Some just wanted to see the Wall, some wanted to touch it, and many were there to find someone's name. We bought the rubbing/tracing supplies at a kiosk near the entrance -- paper and black rubbing compound with instructions. A tour guide at another kiosk gave us a brochure with a map and directions. We made our way, slowly, step by step, down to the first panel.

I was not prepared for the profound sadness I felt upon approaching the first panel. I stopped in my tracks. I felt dizzy. Vertigo. A heaviness. A sudden indescribable stillness. For a few seconds, I stood motionless. I felt my partner tug at my arm, and I did not realize that I had tears in my eyes until he gently handed me a tissue. Although I did not serve, I had not realized how much the war had affected me. Some of my high school friends and family had served, too, and a few had not survived. I pulled myself together and continued the slow walk down the paved promenade. I saw grown men with their hands and fingers touching the wall, crying, sobbing. Women too. Their son, brother, father, friend? Names of souls etched in stone.

With patience and persistence, which is a part of our history as a people, we found the name. There it was: CHRISTOPHER CHARLES FERNANDEZ.

With my partner's assistance, I placed the paper flush with the etched name and began the rubbing process. It took less than a minute. I made two rubbings, just in case. After a moment of prayer and contemplation, we continued down the path of heroes. I was amazed at the large number of Hispanic surnames I saw on that black granite Wall. This made me both sad and yet proud. It took nearly an hour for us to finally reach the end of the last panel. It was an experience I will carry with me for the rest of my life.

That night I called Christina. I said "mission accomplished". I told her I would mail the papers with Chris' name to her immediately. She was very pleased and thanked me profusely. And so, in the end, I was finally able to do something for her after all. It meant as much to me as it did to her. My sweet, kind and loving Christina!

In days to come, who knows what people will say about Christina, or her oldest sister and mother, or about Chris! Were the mistakes they made unforgiveable? Was the Vietnam War a success? It doesn't really matter anymore. I do not know how those who knew them will judge them. I only know that for many years Chris and Christina, inseparable, will remain in my heart. She carries his name with her...today.

Few will remember that they were good people, living good lives, loving each other in life, and, yes, even in death. This much I know: Good people are loving people; and people who love are good people... always.

Ref: www.virturalwall.org

Introduction

Say anything you want to me. But don't lie to me. Lying is a psychological phenomenon. Some people lie a lot, to the level of pathology. Others just tell lies of convenience. Still others commit what is called a white lie, where one simply withholds the truth...mum is the word.

Lies can be damaging and hurtful. Yet, a lie told with good intentions can save a person's life. This is rare, however. Some lies are mundane. "Hey, you look great in that outfit!" Lie!

People lie. Not countries or businesses or religions. People!

When is a lie okay? When it helps people. I deem it to be so!

Cheating is Cheating

Honesty is the best policy.

--- Cervantes (1547-1616) *Don Quixote*

It was my senior year in high school, and I was ready to graduate and move on. Most courses for the last two semesters were electives, except for English Composition I and II. These were requirements, and I was really looking forward to those classes. I liked to write and started when I was in elementary school. I felt I had the talent to write, but not the skills needed to write well. I saw the Composition classes as an opportunity to develop better writing dexterity.

The assignments included homework writing. Our teacher, Mr. Sterne, explained that every week, he would provide us with a topic, and we had one week to write an essay on the topic. There was a limit of 500 to 1000 words. No papers would be accepted after the due date.

The topics varied within a number of themes: politics, religion, society, family, education, environment, the law and morality, and even psychology; current and past issues. I was very excited about the course and I anticipated progress in my writing abilities.

I handed in my first essay. One week later, I got it back. It had a grade of C. Needless to say, I was very disappointed. The following week, I got another C. And the same grade the week after. For a month, nothing but Cs. I began to feel that *maybe writing wasn't my thing*.

One day, Frank Cody, a friend and classmate, and I walked out of class together. He proudly announced that he "...got another A. I've gotten an A on all my papers." I had known Frank for a good number of years, because we were both altar boys at the same church before attending high school. Frank was a jock, and I never thought of him as a writer. I told him that all my essays were graded C. *How did he manage to get all A's on his essays?* I wondered.

"Aw! That's too bad, Dan. Don't give up. It'll get better" he said.

"I don't know. I think Mr. Sterne has something against me. I know that sounds crazy, but I think my papers deserve better than a C."

"Well, I wish I could help you, but..." Frank said apologetically.

"Frank, I've been thinking. Actually, maybe you can help" I said nervously.

"How so?"

"Well, I need to prove to myself that it's me, my writing, and not Mr. Sterne. I don't want to think negatively or wrongly of him. Would you be willing to try something tricky?"

His brow furrowed. "I don't know. It depends."

"Well, what if you and I exchanged essays? You write your paper and I'll write mine. You hand in my paper with your name on it, and I'll hand in your paper with my name on it."

"Oh, I don't know about that. It sounds a little risky, and maybe even illegal."

"Just this once! Please! I want to see what grade we each get on our papers."

Frank hesitated for a second, scratched his head and said "Okay, but just this once. And we can't tell anyone. No one! It's just between you and me. Promise!"

"Yes of course. Look, this is our last year. I don't want to get kicked out of school for cheating. We can pull this off if we just keep it to ourselves. I'll never repeat this to anyone."

Hesitantly, Frank said "Okay. But it's against my moral principles. If it will make you feel better. But Mr. Sterne better never find out."

That week, we got our topic. I wrote my essay; Frank wrote his. He put his name on mine; and I put my name on his. We handed in our papers. They came back the following week. Frank got an A, and I got a C.

Now I was really upset. "I don't understand" I told Frank.

"Yeah, I'm surprised too. Wow!"

"Frank, we have to do this again. I can't be convinced either way unless we try this just one more time. There's got to be an explanation. I feel like I'm being treated unfairly."

Frank also seemed vexed. He shook his head. "You know, you're right. I want to know if this guy has something against you. Let's do it again. But remember, no one must ever find out about this, or we'll be in deep doo-doo. If I get kicked out of school, my parents will kill me."

"Got it! I want to graduate and not get expelled after four years! Thanks, Frank!"

We exchanged papers again, and again forged authorship. I was anxious, as was Frank, to see the grades. The papers were returned to us. Frank got an A; and I got my usual C.

In all fairness, Frank's essays were good...very good. But I thought mine were better. We were both a little dismayed by the results, but we agreed to keep this little ruse between us.

I ended up getting a C+ for the fall course; but did better in Mr. Sterne's spring course. I earned a B in Comp II. I reasoned that my writing simply improved, and I placed no blame on Mr. Sterne. It didn't seem right to confront him and ask about the grade. There was no evidence that he purposely graded my essays as he did. Evaluating essays is about as subjective as writing them. I deemed the composition courses as a learning experience. Putting that first semester behind me, my GPA was only slightly affected by those Cs. Somewhat satisfied that I did as well as I could, I became uncertain about any future writing endeavors.

Soon after graduation, Frank called me. “Hey, guy! We did it! We’re free!”

“Yeah! Now we’re both off to college. I’m looking forward to that. And you?”

“Yup, me too! But, hey. There’s something I need to tell you. We’re good friends, so I hope you’ll understand. But before I tell you, you’ve got to promise that this will be between you and me...and no one else must ever know about it.”

Curious, I said “Okay. I promise. What is it?”

“I never wrote those essays” he said.

There was a long silence. I was in disbelief. “What? What are you saying?”

“I’m saying I never wrote those papers. I paid Fred Rios $1.50, sometimes $2.00 for each essay. Every week, I would give him the topic. He would write the paper, put my name on it, and usually had it ready for me within two or three days.”

“Wait! You had four-eyed Freddie write your homework? That little, nerdy runt?”

“Now be nice, Dan. He’s really very smart. And he saved my butt. I tried writing the first of those assignments and it turned out really awful. No! Writing is not my bag.”

“Well, I’m glad you told me. And Frank, I’ll never tell anyone. I just hope Freddie will keep your secret too. Even though we’ve graduated, there’s nothing to keep Sterne from notifying the college if he finds out.”

“Oh, he’ll never tell anyone. Freddie and I are buds. Anyway, I’ve got something on him too! I found out he’s gay! We both agreed not to share our little secrets.”

Not really surprised, I said “Frank! You just revealed a secret between you and Freddie.”

We both laughed. I concluded *a secret can still be a secret if you share it with friends.*

Nevertheless, having been an altar boy and raised a Catholic, I felt really guilty, and would feel so for many years to come. I had done something dishonest. I had cheated. No one must ever know about this. Excuses were off the table. Self-forgiveness would be difficult if not impossible. I convinced myself *God will forgive me, and that's good enough for me.*

****

Frank and I parted ways, and I had no communication with him for over 25 years. I finished college with a BS in Accounting. My job was satisfying, but not a career. I managed to get my CPA certification while employed as a tax consultant at a small accounting business. In my spare time, I continued to write for my own pleasure. It was more of a hobby which I never took seriously. Writing became my personal self-therapy. Mr. Sterne's grading did not dissuade or deter me from continuing to express myself with the written word.

One day, as was a normal thing for me to do, I stopped at a large bookstore in town to browse and review books I might find interesting. Upon entering the store, I immediately eyed a large display of a book entitled "Texan-French Fusion Cooking". There were about 20 copies, all stacked or standing upright. As I walked past the display, I looked down and couldn't help but notice the author's name on the books: ***François Cote.*** I found this intriguing. Picking up one of the books, I turned to the back inside cover of the jacket. There was a picture of the author -- an obese, bald man whose face looked very familiar to me.

Below the picture, it read "Francois Cote is the *nom de plume* of Frank Cody. Mr. Cody, a Texas gourmet who also considers himself an 'epicurean', provides over 50 recipes ..."

I stopped. My eyes widened in amazement. *Frank wrote a cookbook?*

A young lady working at the bookstore came up and stood next to me. She began to rearrange the books on display.

"I know this guy. I went to high school with him." I said to her. "He looks a lot heavier here, and older. I haven't seen him in over 25 years."

"Well" she said, "looks like he's been eating a lot of the food from his own recipes." She laughed. "You know, he's going to have a book signing here next week. You should come."

On Wednesday, I went to the bookstore with my copy of Frank's book. There he sat at a table. People were lined up to get their copies autographed. When I finally got to Frank, he immediately recognized me.

Excitedly, he stood up. "Dan....oh my goodness! So good to see you. You haven't changed a bit!"

I did not say it, but he certainly had changed; no hair and 100 pounds heavier. "Yeah, good to see you too ***Francois***" I said with emphasis on the French accent! He laughed.

"Hey, I'm almost done here. Don't leave. I want to talk to you before you go. Okay?"

"Sure. I'll be right over there." I sat down in the reading area. It was not long before Frank came over to me.

"Gee, Dan. It's so good to reconnect. Remember" he whispered. "We have a life-long secret; just between you and me. And don't forget poor little Freddie. But, hey! We should get together to go over old times. Are you available Sunday? Hey! You married?"

I hesitated pretending to be thinking about my availability, but I was actually wondering what the urgency was all about. We were friends and classmates in the past, but we weren't really close. Nevertheless, I said "Yeah. Sure. I'm available on Sunday."

Before I could answer his question about being married, he went on...

"Great" he said. "Here's my card with my cell number and address on the back. Come on over for brunch, around ten. My wife makes a fantastic chili soufflé and pancakes ...You know! Look it up:

Chapter 7, page 42 – 'Eggs: Les œufs, Y'all!'"

Frank had said to me "You haven't changed a bit." Apparently, neither had he!

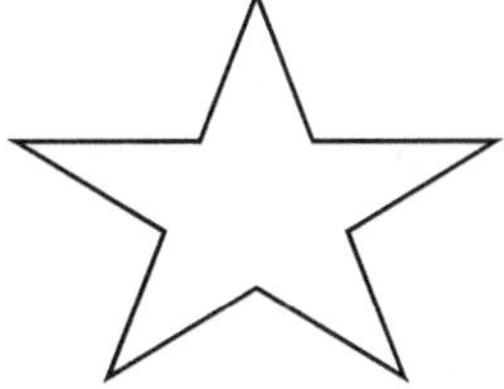

Introduction

Is it a misnomer? Is it an oxymoron? Is it an academic nomenclature? I'm not sure, but I don't understand the term "science fiction." In my mind, it's either science or it's fiction! They are two completely different and separate genres. Maybe I'm being too conservative, too restrictive, and too literal.

In any case, my thoughts have adjusted on this issue since a friend of mine told me this science fiction love story.

CLARA

"Always remember that you are absolutely unique.
Just like everyone else."

-- *Margaret Mead*

In my last year at the university, I remained disappointed. My father would always tell me "Don't expect people to be or do what you want; they will always disappoint you." I was disappointed in myself more than in other people. I had expected to have a serious girlfriend and perhaps a future wife by now. And yet, at 21, I was still alone and in need of companionship. I did have a few "dates." Not much came of those; except that I learned to avoid sorority girls. The reason I came to college was, yes, to get an education and a degree, but mainly I wanted to meet someone. I was thinking long-term relationship.

Then, at the start of my last semester, I got a call from a classmate. He invited me to a study group for a course in technology I was to take that semester. He said it would be a one-time event, hosted by someone who could summarize the entire course in one evening. She was a graduate student by the name of Clara. My friend, Sean, said he would pick me up at 6:00 p.m. on Sunday. I agreed to go.

We arrived at Clara's house on time. There were only 10 students. Clara had set a limit due to time and space constraints. We were directed to a rather large den with cushions on the floor. I was glad we had eaten earlier because there was no food or drink provided.

When Clara entered the room, my heart soared. She was beautiful, an absolute life-size Barbie. She walked with grace and poise, and carried the elegance of a princess. Her eyes beckoned me. When she spoke, her voice was golden, sweet, and clear -- like her name. She was one of a kind – unique, like me.

She began: "Good evening everyone. My name is Clara Santander. Thank you for coming. This evening I am going to provide for you all the information you will need to get an A in Professor Greene's Technology 384 course. The text is *Technology in the Age of Religion*. Any questions before I get started?"

Someone raised his hand and asked "Why *Technology in the Age of Religion*, and not the reverse, *Religion in the Age of Technology*?"

Some of us snickered and quietly groaned. As one of my professors used to say "There are no stupid questions; only stupid people." Clara responded in a gentle and understanding way "You'll have to ask the author about that. It's his book." We all laughed.

But I wasn't paying much attention to the exchange; I was watching Clara with every fiber of obsession that I could muster. I was mesmerized. I was smitten. It was difficult to focus on the topic or on others. For me, she was on stage, and the spotlight was on her.

After a few other questions, Clara began to describe in detail the contents of the book, the specifics of the course, and the expectations of Dr. Greene. She shared the questions he would ask on the tests and final exam. Waving a copy of the Syllabus, she said "you won't need this."

Most of the attendees were feverishly taking notes and trying to write down everything she said. I was still focused on her face, her body, her magnetism. If I were an artist, I would have been drawing her portrait instead of just gaping at her loveliness.

Three hours later, she ended with "I think that covers it. I really don't have anything more to add. Does anyone have any final questions? Ask now because I will not be answering any questions after tonight."

There were no questions because Clara had covered everything we needed to know. Having been fully briefed on the course, everyone began to gather their things and leave. Each student went up to Clara and thanked her personally. I waited till last.

Sean went ahead of me and thanked her with a hug. Clara smiled during the hug and placed her head next to Sean's, facing me. That is when I saw it: a spark in Clara's eye, just on the inside, near the bridge of her nose. Not a glitter! A spark! I was befuddled.

I then approached and hugged her. It was a very nice, long hug. I had read somewhere that a hug that lasts for more than 30 seconds is a love hug. Was she also aware of this? I thanked her. She smiled. I said "My name is Paco, Paco Pecina. Can I call you sometime? Not for questions about the course. But maybe we can go out for dinner or something."

She nodded. "Give me your number, and I'll call you if I get some time." I complied.

On the way home, I kept thinking about Clara. She did not disappoint me nor did I feel let down by her "coolness". I wondered if she was 'the one' I'd been hoping for. Could she? Would she? I was heart-pounding excited about the whole experience.

Sean, who was driving me home, turned to me. "What 'cha thinking? Is it Clara?"

"Yeah! How'd you guess?"

"Everyone falls for her when they first meet her. I did...at first."

"Really? Yeah, well there's just one thing that bothers me. When she was hugging you, I noticed a .... well, a spark in her eye. Not a glitter, but an actual spark. Was I just imagining it?"

"No. It was definitely a spark. That happens when she is attracted to someone. It's like an electrical attraction."

"Wait! What?" I was a little stunned by his response. I did not know how to react. I just stared at the road ahead. I must have looked dumbfounded. There was something eerie about this. I couldn't put my finger on it. My curiosity grew.

Sean laughed, and then he smiled. "She's an android, dummy! And her full name is Clara Four-Eleven Ampersand."

"An android? Are you kidding me? She's not real? What the....."

Sean interrupted "Hey, no need to panic. She's real. At least she's not a cyborg. Actually, she's better than human. How do you think she knew so much about the text and the course? She has at least 100 books programmed into her database. She's a walking, talking Wikipedia. And – very important – she has emotions. She is a sentient organism. And, she likes you."

I was still beside myself. "Yeah, but she aint human."

"She's better than human" Sean yelled! "Humans are annoying and a lot of trouble."

"So what's the difference between a cyborg and an android?"

"A cyborg is a human with robotic, mechanical parts added to the body to expand its capabilities and functions. It's half human and half machine. An android is a robot that has been made to look and behave and think, and even feel, just like a human being. Anatomically, a robot can be almost human. Clara is human and the perfect person. If she calls you to go out, go!"

"So why don't you date her?"

"I'm already engaged. You know that. And, I aint messin' around with someone else!"

"Well," I said, "I'll have to think about this *bizarre* situation. I'm really confused."

When I got back to my dorm, I was still befuddled and began to question my own thoughts and feelings. Could this be a temporary obsession? Love at first sight kinda thing? Raised a Catholic, and an altar boy to boot, what would my priest and family think? I pondered whether or not to pursue this whole notion ... this Clara thing. What would be in store for me if I did? Can she be intimate? Surely she is incapable of bearing children! What kind of relationship would we have? Bewilderment led to a restless attempt to fall asleep. Thoughts of me with an android swirled in my head. *How crazy is that!*

Should I worry about what others might think of me and Clara together? It's none of their business. But that's a naïve consideration. Of course it matters what others think. We would or could not live in isolation. And why am I asking myself all these questions? I just met her tonight...and with a group of other students. I doubt she will even remember me! *Caramba!*

I'm not sure how long I slept, but I suddenly awoke. My slumber interrupted, I looked over at the clock-radio on my nightstand. It read 4:11 am ... *am* as in ampersand. This was very strange and unsettling. I was slightly dazed as the green digital display blurred.

I thought *maybe I just need to pee*. I got out of bed and made my way into the bathroom and switched on the light. I sat on the commode. I could not pee. I made a mental note to call my doctor in the morning. I hoped I didn't have another pseudo case of nocturia.

I stood up from the commode and tapped the light switch to *off*.

In the dark, I turned to face the mirror. My eyes were *on*.

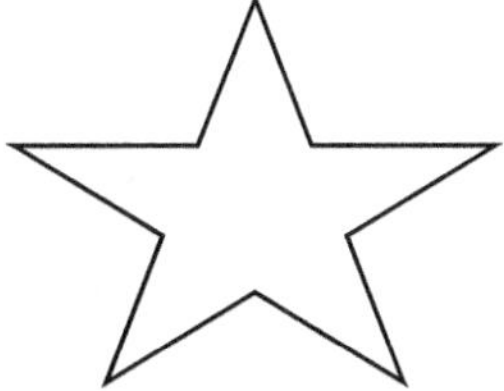

Introduction

I have a great deal of respect for journalists – in print, in the news (on TV), and those who make documentaries. They both inform and, at some level, entertain. I am impressed with their ability to talk to people (interviews) and get the most out of their subjects. This is a talent and a skill.

Many journalists are also celebrities, in a way. TV journalists must be attractive, photogenic, articulate, and have projecting personalities. If I were a journalist, I might want to give the teller of this next story a few tips. For sure, don't swim in muddy waters and stay in your lane.

Hapless Happy

What is given by the gods more desirable than a happy hour?

Catullus (85 – 54 B.C.) Odes

I am proud to have received a degree from the University of Missouri, School of Journalism. It is a prestigious school ranked in the top ten among comparable universities. Graduates include well known and recognized journalists in print and on A/V broadcasts such as ESPN, CNN, FOX News, and PBS, e.g., Jim Lehrer. Over the past 50 years there have been more than 25 Pulitzer Prize winners. I was in good company. But I had no experience outside of the school newspaper.

Soon after my graduation, a friend and classmate, Blaine, stopped me and asked about my plans. I explained that I was not sure yet. I was financially secure and not in any hurry to get a job. He was returning to his hometown of Houston and already had a job lined up with the Houston Chronicle. He often reminded me that Walter Cronkite grew up in Houston and developed his journalistic skills there and at the University of Texas.

"You will need a little experience outside of school to be able to get a good-paying job." He explained.

"Of course, but I'm on the fence as to where and how to begin." I said.

"Well, allow me to make a suggestion. There is a town in Texas called Happy."

I chuckled! "You aren't serious are you?"

"Oh, I'm serious alright! Happy, Texas, population around 700. It's in northwest Texas, in the Texas Panhandle, just south of Amarillo. You'd love it."

"And why would you suggest that place? I don't want to live there. Besides, I'm already happy."

"Listen to me. About two years ago, a man went missing...disappeared. He has never been located. Everybody in Happy knew him, but nobody knows what happened to him."

"And you think I should go there...to do what?"

"Go there and put your skills to work. Interview the locals. Find out all you can about him. Maybe if you poke around and do enough digging, you might be able to solve the mystery of his disappearance. The local officials were unable to do it. Maybe you can."

"Hmm! That sounds tempting, and interesting...and challenging."

"This would put a feather in your cap and it would look great on your resume. You can write an article on how you solved the mystery of this missing guy. What do ya' think?"

"Well, do you know this guy's name?"

"His name is Hap, Hap Larkin. And he's been missing for about two years or more."

"What? Wait! Hap Larkin? Hap in Happy? Come on, Blaine!"

"Well his real name is or was Henry Larkin, but everybody, including the newspaper, called him Hap."

"So he disappeared. How do they know if he's even alive? He could be dead."

"That's where you come in. You could solve the mystery. You need to find out what happened to Hap. Just go there and start asking questions. Somebody has to know something."

I was intrigued by the idea, but at the same time I thought it ridiculous of me to go to Happy and try to make something out of nothing. The local officials had come up empty. I thought *How could I do any better than they?* Nevertheless, the next morning I began making arrangements for the long drive to Happy. *Crazy? Maybe!* I wondered *But what if I succeeded? Now that would be something!*

My plan was not to spend more than a few nights there. Using my GPS, I drove west through Kansas City into Kansas, and then southwest across the Sunflower State. I admired the flowing flint hills and the lush, flat grazing fields and farmlands along the way. It was a pleasant drive. By evening I had reached Liberal, Kansas. [Now there's an oxymoron for you!] Liberal is a "cute" town with friendly people. It is where the "Land of Oz" exhibit is housed. There is a replica of Dorothy's house and the Yellow Brick Road leading to the Wizard's hideout. Every year there is a Wizard of Oz festival. I'd have to think about that one.

I was tired that night, but still pulled out my laptop in my motel room and looked up 'Hap'. Apparently, other than it being a nick-name for Henry or Harry, the word itself is Scot-Anglo-Saxon-German meaning luck, chance, and fortune. I became even more curious as to Hap's fate.

Driving south, I crossed two panhandles side by side – Oklahoma and Texas panhandles. I stopped at a burger joint in Amarillo for lunch. There I met a man who noticed my out-of-state plates. He was friendly and seemed to want to talk to someone.

"Welcome to the Lone Star State. I see your plate says Missouri. What's Missouri's motto?"

"Show Me! The Show Me State."

"That's a weird motto! What does that mean?"

"It means you need to show me proof, evidence, facts, concrete support of what you say; not just opinion, conjecture, or assumption."

"Sounds too complicated to me. I like Lone Star. Nice and simple. So where you headed?"

"I'm on my way to Happy, but I'm a little short on time, so I've got to get going."

His eyes widened. "Happy? Huh! Aint' nothin' goin' on there!" he opined.

While in Amarillo, I managed to locate a copy of "AAA TourBook Guide – Texas". But I was disappointed that Happy was not even on the list of cities and towns in the book.

The drive from Amarillo to Happy is nothing to talk or write home about. Upon entering the city limits, I saw the billboard off the road. It wasn't very big and appeared to be hand painted. In large, bold letters it read "WELCOME TO HAPPY, TEXAS. THE TOWN WITHOUT A FROWN." I had to grin after seeing that sign. I soon found a small motel on the side of the highway and settled in for a quiet evening.

The following morning I went to the front office. I asked the desk clerk if she knew anything about Hap Larkin. She said she had heard of him, but she didn't know anything about him. She suggested I ask at the local diner. That was a great idea because I was really hungry for breakfast. I headed to 'Joy's Family Diner'. It was only five-minutes away.

I sat down and the waitress came to my table and handed me a menu. She was wearing a nametag that said 'Joy". She filled my cup with coffee without asking me.

"Do you own this diner?" I asked.

"No. My mother does; and before her, my grandmother. That's where I get my name."

"Oh, I see." She left and returned after a few minutes.

"What 'cha gonna have, honey?" She poured more coffee into my cup.

"Oh, just a couple of scrambled eggs, bacon, some potatoes, and wheat toast."

She pointed to the menu. "Number 7. That's what you want. I call it Seventh Heaven." She laughed at her own joke and scooted back to the kitchen.

After I had my fill of nourishment, she returned. "Anything else, honey?"

"Yes. Do you know anything about Hap Larkin? I understand he's missing."

"Hap? Oh yeah. I knew Hap. He hasn't been around for a long time. Some folks say he disappeared or went away. But even though he came here a lot, he would sometimes not show up for weeks or even months. So I'm not surprised. He'll show up some day. He always ordered the same thing...every day... pancakes, huevos rancheros, and coffee. Same thing every time."

"So you don't think anything nefarious has happened to him? You think he'll reappear?"

"If you're asking if I'm worried about him, no I'm not. Hap's a survivor. He'll be back."

At about that time I heard some loud laughing from a boisterous group in a large half-moon booth at the other end of the diner. I paid my bill and went up to their table.

"Excuse me for interrupting, but my name is Steven de Lara, and I'm a journalist. I'm interested in the disappearance of Hap Larkin. Can any of you provide me with any information?"

There was an eerie silence at the table. Finally, a middle-aged man with wire-rim glasses said "We don't know nothin' about Hap. One day he just up and goes, and he aint been seen since."

"Do you know who I might be able to talk to, someone who might have been close to him?"

A very large, dare I say obese, woman, whose body took up a quarter of the seating, raised her hand and said "Yeah. You need to speak to the Reverend Funston at the First Baptist Church down the street. He was pretty tight with Hap." She pointed in the direction of the church.

"...Just about two blocks down, at the corner, can't miss it."

"Thank you, ma'am. I'll head down to talk to him now."

"Good! Tell the preacher that Side-Car Sally sent you." Everyone at the table laughed.

The man with the glasses chimed in "You might also check with the Sheriff. He's the one who took the reports and did the investigation."

Of course, why didn't I think of that?

The church was plain and simple and probably, in its earlier years, white on the outside. I entered the main door. Churches have their own unique smell. [I recalled the smell of the church where I grew up and served as an altar boy]. Once my eyes adjusted to the darkness, I saw the figure of a man sitting in the back pew.

"Reverend Funston?"

He turned. "Yes?"

"Sir, Side-car Sally sent me. My name is Steven de Lara and I'm working on an article regarding the disappearance of Hap Larkin. I was told you were close to him."

"Hap was a wonderful man. He would do anything for anybody in need. He came here often; and yet, there were times when I wouldn't see him for weeks or months."

"Do you know if he had any family here? Was he married? Was he born here?"

"No to all those questions. I don't recall when he got here, but he was already a grown man when I met him. I'm sure he never married. But the rumor was that he had a daughter in New Mexico. He would go visit her every now and then.

"He would come here and help out; volunteer to do things for nothing...no pay. He repaired all the pews so that they wouldn't squeak or be loose off the floor. Once,

I came into the church and he was mopping the floor. I asked him why, and he said 'Oh, I was just out back and saw this bucket and mop and decided to swab the entire church floor. The house of God should have clean floors. When I'm done here, I think I'll clean those windows.'"

"Sounds like he was very industrious! Did he have a full-time job elsewhere?

"No not really. He used to go out to the Gleeson ranch and do some branding for cash. Other than him coming here to do work around the church, I don't know what else he did. I never asked. He was private and I respected that. If he wanted me to know something, he'd tell me."

"Of course! What do you think happened to Mr. Larkin?"

"I have no idea, young man. I don't think about it much either. I figure, he'll show up."

"Even though it's been over two years?" No response. "Well, thank you for your help. You've been most kind. Do you know of anyone else I can talk to?"

"Like I said...the Gleeson ranch." Changing the subject, he asked "By the way, do you know the secret to being happy?"

"No, not really."

"Well, it aint livin' in Happy, Texas. To praise and serve the Lord. That's happiness! Hap knew that! He lived it."

Before lunch I made my way out to the Gleeson ranch. Mr. Gleeson was sitting on his porch when I drove up. He was wearing a cowboy hat and smoking a pipe.

"Howdy" he said.

"Hello. My name is Steven de Lara, and I'm in need of any information on Hap Larkin and what you might know about his absence."

"Don't know." Pulling on his goatee, he added "I haven't seen him in some time. He used to come here and help me brand cattle for the other ranchers in the area. I paid him well...cash. He worked hard, and at the end of the day, he thanked me, pocketed his money and left. Strange fellow, Hap!"

"Well then, can you direct me to anyone else who can maybe fill in the gaps? I'm having a hard time getting any information about him from anyone I've talked to."

"Let me put it this way, young man. He wouldn't be doing this for you. He'd leave you to your own affairs. He'd say 'not my concern.'"

"I hear he may be in New Mexico, and that he may have a daughter there. Do you think he's there? Or, aren't you a little worried that something bad might have happened to him?"

"What if something bad did happen to him? Aint nothing I can do about it. As for New Mexico, you should ask that waitress at the diner, Joy. She and him were real close.

"Look, you seem like a nice fella'. If Hap wanted us to know his whereabouts, he'd let us know. And that's that!"

Again disappointed, I thanked him and walked back to my car. Before driving away, I heard him yell "Hey! Talk to Tommy at 'The Laughing Cow.' He's usually there after 6 o'clock."

"Okay. Do I just ask for Tommy? Does he work there?"

"No. He drinks there. You can't miss him. He'll be the only black guy in there. And he's blind."

Before going to talk to Tommy, I stopped at the Sheriff's office and inquired about Hap. He seemed very reluctant and said "It's a cold case and I consider it closed. That's all I can tell you." I asked if he had a picture of Hap. He said he did not because there is no record of an ID or a birth certificate or even a driver's license. He verified "I checked with the Department of Motor Vehicles (DMV), and they have no record of him. I'm sure he used to drive an old pick up, but I never bothered to check his license. He seemed innocent enough."

The office which published the news about Hap abutted the Sheriff's office, so I stopped in there. The old gentleman sitting at the roll-top desk said he printed what he knew about Hap almost three years ago. "I got no more to say about it. We don't know any more. Talk to the Sheriff."

"I did. And he had nothing to add."

"Well there you are." The old man kept coughing and holding one hand to his throat. A half-smoked cigarette was between the fingers of his other hand. More coughing. "Do you know the meaning of happiness? (*Not again!*) Good health. Health and Happiness go together. All you need to be happy is your health. Remember that. You have a nice day, now. God bless!"

After dinner, I went out to search for Tommy. The Laughing Cow was an old-time saloon with wooden floors, and a hitching post out front. I saw a black man sitting at a corner table with a beer and a shot glass in front of him.

"Tommy?"

"Yes. Tommy Gladden. Who's asking?"

"My name is Steven de Lara, and I was wondering if you could help me with some information. It's about Hap Larkin. I'm trying to track him down."

"No you're not. You're trying to dig up dirt, or to use your word 'information' as to his whereabouts. Your reputation precedes you, sir. I got nothing against you, Mr. de Lara. But, Hap hasn't been around for quite a while. He'll be back in his own time. No need to broadcast about him. You need to see things from his perspective."

"Well then, give me your perspective."

He hesitated. "Hap was a really good man. He'd come in here and buy me drinks. We'd sit here and talk. I never asked him personal questions. We never talked about others. He never commented on my blindness. Do you understand? Man has ears, but he sometimes hears not. Man has eyes, but he sometimes sees not. I can't see, but your voice helps me envision you. I'd say you are in your late 20s, about five feet and nine inches, and you aint from around here."

"You are right on all points. Why is the disappearance of Hap Larkin such a mystery? Don't you want to know? Wasn't he a friend of yours?"

"I'm curious, but I don't need to know. Hap is gone right now; but he may return. This I know. If he were to come in here and sit down in front of me and not say a word, I'd know it be him."

"I'm sorry if I sounded intrusive. I don't mean to be. I'm a journalist and I write. I wanted to write about Hap and possibly even help to solve the mystery of his disappearance.

"Okay. I can see, excuse the pun; I can see that you are persistent in efforts to find out more about Hap. But I can't help you. There's one other person you might talk to if you haven't already. That's Hap's barber. Ruben Feliz. He owns 'The Cut n Run' on Main."

"Thank you. Sorry to bother you. Can I buy you a drink?"

"Sure. If you'll stay and drink one with me."

I did.

After a few drinks, it was getting late. So I went back to the motel with plans to meet Ruben at his barbershop the next morning; then maybe head home. I didn't seem to be getting anywhere, and didn't want to waste any more time on this project. I needed to bring it to an end.

The following day, I drove to Ruben's barber shop. He was just finishing a cut. I introduced myself and asked about Hap.

"Hap? That no good son-of-a bench. He owes me for about 20 haircuts and shaves. Course I don't expect to ever get paid, but I'd sure like to give him a piece of my mind."

"Do you have any idea what happened to Hap? Could he be dead or alive? You think maybe he was kidnapped? Do you have any theory as to his fate?"

"Look here, Mr. de Lara! Back in 1999 Hollywood released a movie called "Happy, Texas". Those snobs didn't even have the courtesy of filming it here. It was filmed in California. Our town is not a circus and our people are not clowns to be mocked and made fun of. Journalists are almost as annoying as Hollywood folk. You think you're the first to come here trying to solve the mystery of Hap Larkin's disappearance? You're not! I'm sorry, but I can't help you. I don't know what happened to Hap. And I don't need to know. Ignorance is Bliss. Go back home and look for another story to write about."

"I did not know that there were others here before me. I apologize."

I persisted. "Some folks say he went to live with his daughter in New Mexico. What about that?"

"I heard that too. But I don't think he'd move there without Joy. They were intimate, you know."

"No I didn't know that. Do you think Hap's daughter would know his whereabouts?"

"Of course you'll need to ask her. Won't you? Good luck finding her."

I headed for the door.

"You want a haircut? I'll give you an out-of-town discount."

"No, thank you...But let me ask you one last question. If Hap came in here right now and wanted a haircut, would you give him one, knowing he owes you for 20 previous unpaid cuts?"

Ruben hesitated and continued to clean a large green comb with a towel. He put the comb in a tin that read 'reusable'.

"Yes I would. In a heartbeat! And let me tell you somethin' else. Hap was not a bad person. He was very likable, even if he was a little eccentric. He didn't pay his bills, but if you asked him for a favor, consider it done. They don't make men like him anymore. Hap gave us all a little happiness. Ya know, he had a philosophy about being happy, Mr. de Lara. It's not being angry or pissed off at people. It's not being bored or depressed. "Happiness is a 'subtle emotion' he once said. No enduring revenge; no holding a grudge. Happiness is having the strength to forgive. 'Forgive and let go!' That was his expression.

"Yes, I'd cut Hap's hair, shave him, and wish him the best. You have a good day, sir."

"You too, Mr. Feliz." I headed back to the motel to spend my last night in Happy.

The next morning I checked out and then stopped at Joy's Family Diner. Joy was there and came to my table. She was a pretty woman in her mid-thirties.

"I see you're back." She poured coffee in my cup without asking.

"Yes. I wanted to ask again about Hap. I have since learned that you and he were close."

Her smile changed to a flat countenance. Her glow faded. A tear escaped its hiding place and settled on her cheek.

"Yes, we were very close. But like I said, he would sometimes come every day; and then only show up once a week, or once a month, or like now...I haven't seen him in over two years."

"I'm sorry if I upset you. You must miss him terribly. Do you have a picture of him? The sheriff and the news editor said there is no picture."

"No. The only picture I have of him is in my mind, in my imagination, in my memory. He didn't like his picture being taken."

"I see. Just curious, but what did he look like?"

She stared at me affectionately. "He looked a little like you...only taller.

"So what's it gonna be? For breakfast."

"I'll have ... pancakes, huevos rancheros, and coffee" I said sadly.

She pointed to the menu again and said "Number 9. I call it Cloud Nine." And she laughed at her own joke.

And so after breakfast I said good bye and headed home, from Happy to Missouri, with thoughts of both regret and unfinished business.

Driving north, I had a lot of time to ponder on Hap and Happy, Texas, and the people I met there. I couldn't get Hap out of my mind. I felt like I had failed him; and failed myself. Yet, something gnawed at me. *What were the missing pieces of the puzzle?*

Then it struck me.

Maybe Hap Larkin is not missing; nor did he disappear. Maybe Hap Larkin does not exist or never did. And even if he did, he only existed in the minds and hearts of the people of Happy.

I could not help but think of my psychology teacher describing symptoms of mental illness. He said that hallucinations occur when people experience a sensory response in the absence of a sensory stimulation. A person sees or hears what no one else can see or hear. Delusions are beliefs in the absence of reality. For example, I believe I'm a Nobel Prize winner. Not real; I am not. Yet upon closer examination, one can entertain the idea of a separate reality; an alternate reality. To the delusional person, his beliefs are as real as reality is to everyone else. Hallucinations are real, very real. Delusions are a separate reality...and very real.

I pride myself at being a skilled observer of people and their behavior. I pay attention to what they do or don't do; and how they do it. I examine what people say or don't say; and how they say it. At the same time, I try not to be judgmental, although that is a natural response.

Do I think that the people of Happy are delusional? Maybe! But who am I to challenge their reality? The people of Happy believe that Hap Larkin exists. Maybe he did at one time. But beliefs can often override the facts. They believe that Hap is alive and will return some day.

In spite of my 'Show Me' nature, I was beginning to understand the perspective of the residents of Happy. One can experience real happiness, even in the absence of its reality.

It turns out that Hap Larkin is as elusive as happiness itself. I needed to take <u>MY</u> reality and go home.

And one more thing! Their belief in the existence of Hap gave them purpose; gave meaning to their lives; made them unique and special. I have learned that we have to believe in something to be happy; even if believing in a ghost makes one happy.

*****

And yet....

Wouldn't it be a shock to me if Hap Larkin actually did one day show up in Happy? So much for my academic theories!

Alone in my car, I said aloud "Hap Larkin, wherever you are, please come home. Your friends in Happy miss you!"

Introduction

You can't help everyone. You can't rescue everyone. You can't put out every fire that comes your way. But...You can try. And sometimes your attempts to help others can backfire. I cannot count the number of times I have extended myself to others, only to have them react with 'mind your own business or 'I don't need your help'; or just ignore my efforts.

Of course this is not always true. You've heard the expression "No good deed goes unpunished." Well, I believe that 99% of good deeds are rewarded (more or less). There have been more times when people respond positively and seem to appreciate your concern with kindness and empathy. Attempt to recognize gratitude. It's often very subtle.

The following story, as told to me by a colleague, caught my attention. Choice is an interesting word to me. "Chose what's behind door 1, door 2, or door 3." But one does not really know for sure what is behind any of the doors. Sadly, for some, having to choose between any given door is not a choice. And yet, choose a door you must.

Rex for 72 Hours

Sympathy is a virtue much cultivated by those who are morally uplifted by the sufferings and misfortunes of others.

-- Oscar Hammling

Although I am now retired, I began my career as a staff psychologist at an in-patient mental health facility in central Texas. The facility had 4 units, each named after a Texas wild flower. I was assigned to the Bluebonnet Unit. Every day began with the unit Morning Report, usually given by the charge nurse. For many years during my tenure on the Bluebonnet Unit (BU) that was Ramona T., RN.

Many of the patients had severe mental illnesses and behavioral problems. Most had "major" diagnoses, and some were in acute, or temporary, crises situations. I soon began to appreciate my work and felt satisfied helping my patients advance toward stability. With appropriate medication and therapeutic treatment, most were able to go home and resume their lives outside the facility. They became better prepared to manage their mental and emotional health issues.

Not all of them stayed out of the facility. There were some, the chronically ill, for whom living independently outside the structured organization was too much for them, and for their loved ones, to deal with. They were better served by staying in a confined, controlled environment. After discharge, circumstances often forced them to return for continued treatment.

Upon admission to the facility, whether voluntarily or involuntarily, each new patient had to undergo a 72-hour evaluation period to determine whether or not they met the criteria for continued, on-going treatment. To meet the retention criteria, the individual had to be considered a possible danger to oneself and/or to others. There were usually other extenuating factors which also needed to be addressed. For example, the patient might have physical health issues. And, sometimes family would not take the individual back home. Or the patient was indigent and had no income to maintain one's own living situation, such as homelessness. If the patient did not meet the long-term criteria, he or she would be discharged within or after 72 hours.

Tuesday, eight a.m. – Morning Report

I had been working at this institution for more than 10 years, when one spring morning, Ramona reported about a young man who had been admitted the night before. She handed me and the psychiatrist, Dr. Mary Russell, copies of the Intake Form.

His name was Reymundo Bonilla, a single 21 year old male, a recent college graduate.

"If the last name sounds familiar," Ramona explained, "it's because the family owns the Tortilla Bonilla Factory as well as the Sopapilla Bonilla Bakery. As you may know, they are contracted by the largest grocery store chain in Texas, and so you might say they are not hurting financially. Reymundo, who goes by Rex, is the only son of the owner and family patriarch."

The family had driven over 50 miles the previous night to bring Rex to the facility. Ramona didn't report much more about him except to say that he was cooperative, but behaving strangely, manically. I scheduled to interview him soon after reading the Intake information.

Monday, eight p.m. -- Admission & Intake from the night before

According to the Intake Form: "Three weeks ago, Mr. Bonilla and his fiancée, Lisa, drove to Laredo, Texas in order to cross over into Nuevo Laredo, Mexico. Once in Mexico, they went to pick up a wedding dress for Lisa. One week earlier, she had selected the dress she liked and was fitted for it. She also left a deposit. She chose this Boutique in Nuevo Laredo because Rex's sister had used it. The workmanship was of good quality, and it was also less expensive. Once across the border, they went directly to the Dress Shop.

"After trying on the dress for the last time, Lisa and Rex were impressed with the finished garment. Satisfied with the dress, including veil and gloves, the seamstress then neatly and carefully folded and arranged the dress with matching accessories into a white box. They paid the balance in cash and left.

"They then headed back to the border crossing. After passing through customs and immigration, they were eager to get home and show the families Lisa's wedding ensemble. With Rex driving, they headed north on IH-35, The Purple Heart Trail.

"There was a tragic accident. Their car was forced off the road and overturned several times. Twenty-year old Lisa was killed.

"The family reported that Rex was only slightly injured. He did not drink, or smoke, or use drugs. The police report stated that the other two cars involved had been racing down the highway. The report said that the other drivers were at fault, and that Rex had done nothing to cause the accident. It was unsettling to the first responders who noted the large white box, torn open and still partially containing the wedding ensemble, scattered across the highway and roadside.

"Rex was seen at a local hospital for precautionary reasons and then released. While he was at the hospital, he was told of Lisa's fate. When the family got home, they report, he began to behave strangely. He did not show any signs of grief. He would not stop talking 'nonsense' and was acting as if he were drunk or on drugs, slurring his words, moving about aimlessly, and acting "silly." He also would not eat or go to sleep; up all hours of the night talking aloud to himself. He had been behaving in this manner for nearly two weeks. The family physician prescribed some sleeping medication and told the family that his mania would be temporary.

"This morning, the family found him in his room unresponsive. Rex had apparently overdosed on the sedatives. The family concluded that this was a suicide attempt.

"They rushed him to a local hospital. After the receiving staff pumped his stomach and stabilized him, the ER physician recommended that they bring Rex to our facility for further evaluation. Not knowing what else to do, the family followed his advice and brought Rex in just before eight p.m. this evening. He is cooperative, but mildly disoriented.

"Supplemental information is attached, including a report from the hospital ER..."

Tuesday, one p.m. – First Session

Rex was escorted into my office by a psychiatric aide.

"This is Mr. Rex Bonilla." The aide said as he handed me additional paperwork.

I extended my hand "Nice to meet you, Mr. Bonilla. Please have a seat."

He looked tired and stressed; thin, maybe underfed, and somewhat unkempt. He scanned the room, and then focused on the paperwork on my desk.

"My name is Dr. Davila. I'm a staff Psychologist here. Can you tell me what happened to bring you to this place?"

"My sister and mother brought me here. They think there's something wrong with me."

"Please, tell me more about that."

"Well, you see. I didn't want to kill myself. I just wanted to bring an end to this life."

"What exactly did you do?"

"So, I took some pills. A lot of pills. Sleeping pills. I wanted to go to sleep and never wake up."

His eyes were downcast and began to swell. He seemed nervous and fidgety. Still mildly hyper, he kept moving and continually standing up and then sitting down for no apparent reason.

"And why did you want to go to sleep and never wake up?"

"I told you, I wanted to end my life."

"But what happened that made you want to end your life?"

"Nothing happened. My life happened."

"Was it because of the accident?"

"Which accident? The one where I killed my fiancée? Or the one where I tried to kill myself?"

"Rex! May I call you Rex?"

"Sure, whatever!"

"So, I still don't understand the need to end your life. You seem like an intelligent young man, a college graduate, and with a caring family."

"How would you feel if you were responsible for your fiancée's death?" he mumbled.

"I guess I'd feel very guilty, sad, and regretful. Rex, I'm so sorry about what happened. Your grief must be overwhelming."

"I can't cry; just don't feel like crying. I couldn't even find the strength to go to her funeral."

"Lisa's funeral?"

"Yes! You see, I can't even say her name."

"Okay. Well, I see Dr. Russell has you on some medication. It may take a few days for the benefits to take effect. She seems to think that you have P.T.S.D. Do you know what that is?"

"Of course I do. I might have that. I don't know. I don't know what's going on with me right now. I just feel really bad. I don't understand any of it. Why did this have to happen?"

"Where it concerns accidents, that's a normal question. More importantly, what happens next? What do you do now? I can tell you this, suicide is not an option. It's a permanent solution to a temporary problem. I'm confident that you will work your way through this. Are you?"

"Confident? No. I'm not confident right now. You know, doctors don't understand everything."

"Yes, you're right about that. But I do care that you get better. I may not totally understand, but I do sympathize with your situation. I'm here to help...if I can."

I didn't want to upset Rex, so the rest of the session I focused on building rapport and trust. I allowed Rex to talk about his school days, family, and friends, anything other than Lisa and the accident. These mundane topics helped him to relax and breathe normally.

By the end of the session, I felt that we had made some progress. I told him I would see him again the next day. He was okay with that. After the session, I entered my progress notes into his computer record, using the SOAP method – an acronym meaning Subjective and

Objective observations, Assessment (diagnoses), and Plan.

Tuesday, 6 p.m. – Sister's Visit

"Sorry to bother you, Dr., but Rex Bonilla's sister is here to see you", said the aide.

"That's okay. Hi! I'm Dr. Davila. How can I help you...Ms....."

"Turner, Rita Turner. I'm here to talk to you about Rex."

"Good to meet you. Please have a seat."

She immediately began to tell me about Rex. He was her younger brother. He was a really great guy. He was smart and athletic, was very popular in school, and well liked by everyone. He and Lisa met in high school and soon became "a thing". Lisa was also well liked and popular. Sometime last year, Lisa announced to Rex that she wanted to get married, and Rex, at first reluctant, eventually agreed. So they set a date for the following summer.

The family could not have been happier. Rita was married and was pregnant with her second child. But it was important that Rex get married to carry on the family name. Their father owned and managed both the tortilla factory and the bakery. It was their father's expectation that when he retired, Rex would take over and run both businesses.

"Rex is not his real name. His birth name was Rey, or Reymundo, after my uncle. Rey, as you know, means King in Spanish. In high school, Rex read the story of Oedipus Rex. Rex means King in Latin. He didn't like the story so much, but he liked the name, so he started calling himself Rex. It didn't take long before everybody started calling him Rex.

"We have some concern. We know Rex will get better, but we want to help him find someone to replace Lisa, and soon. He needs to let go of the memory of Lisa and the accident."

I could not believe what I was hearing. There seemed to be little concern for Rex or for Lisa's death. Rita and her family were more concerned about marriage, children, and the businesses. She was trying to appear pragmatic. She hoped that treatment would result in things getting back to "normal" and that Rex would be himself again and be ready to move on.

"He needs to get on with his life. For the sake of the family, he needs to put this behind him. And, the sooner the better. The overdose of pills might have been his way to get attention. Rex, being younger and the only boy in the family, is spoiled and is used to getting his way; -- always has been."

I explained that the psychiatrist gave him a diagnosis of PTSD, with symptoms of depression and anxiety. I added that Rex was also suffering from survivor's guilt.

"He will get over that once he finds someone to take Lisa's place. You'll help with that. Won't you?" she asked with a cold stare.

I told her that I would do my best, but that any improvement or progress would have to come from Rex in his own way and in his own time.

She acknowledged that, thanked me, and left. Nevertheless, I felt uneasy with our conversation, which was to me in a form of "unfinished business."

Wednesday, eight a.m. – Morning Report

At Morning Report, Ramona said that Tuesday night Rex had gotten into an altercation with another resident. It seems that they were standing in the medication line, and Rex was arguing with the nurse about his prescriptions. An aggressive male patient standing behind him became agitated and pushed Rex out of the line. Rex retaliated and grabbed the man by the neck and threw him down. The aides separated them and gave emergency medication, a sedative by injection, to the other man. The patient who pushed Rex had a reputation for aggression and violence.

"There were no serious injuries." Ramona added. "Rex was 'undisturbed' by the incident, and he was cooperative with staff."

Wednesday, 9:15 a.m. – Second Session

This morning, Rex seemed somewhat calmer than the day before. He was not as fidgety or edgy, and eye contact had improved.

"So how exactly can you help, doc?" he started off.

"I hope I can offer some guidance, some direction; maybe make suggestions as to where we can go from here."

I added, "You know your sister came by yesterday afternoon. She wanted to talk about plans for your future."

"I know. They seem to be more concerned about my future than I am. I just want to get through today; like one day at a time. I'm not feeling optimistic, but my mind tells me that, as you said, I can work my way out of this eventually."

"That makes sense to me. Rex, I may not completely understand what you are experiencing right now, but, as I said yesterday, I can sympathize with what you are having to deal with. I can't imagine what you must be faced with at this moment. So, I want you to share with me whatever is on your mind, without censorship, freely and openly. Help me to understand you, in the here and now."

For the next 40 minutes, Rex shared many superficial thoughts. In all that time, he never mentioned Lisa, the accident, his sister, or his family. I surmised that he just wanted to keep all the negative thoughts out of his consciousness. He talked about friends and unrelated events, and things that made him feel content, accepted, and safe. He avoided talking about anything unpleasant. I allowed him to do this, for now.

I asked him about the altercation the day before.

"What happened last night?"

"Oh, I guess you might call it a little scuffle. It was just some crazy guy trying to start trouble. It was nothing. I'm okay. It's over."

Rex thanked me and left. He seemed more lucid and grounded to me. It was too early to tell if we were making any real progress. We would have to get past the superficial topics. And yet, there was a definite change in the right direction, a positive change. I noted these changes in his computer record.

Wednesday, 12:30 p.m. -- Consult

At noon, I met a colleague for lunch at the Bow Thai Restaurant. He was an older, more experienced practitioner who covered the Winecup Unit. I often consulted with him about specific patients. When not at the facility and in a public environment, we made sure not to mention names and to keep our conversations private, for confidentiality purposes.

"So what's up at B.U.?"

I shared with him all I could about Rex's case. He told me that Rex was holding back, avoiding emotional issues. He felt that Rex was getting pressure from his sister and father to accommodate their plans for him. He surmised that Rex was "stuck" between their wants and his own unfulfilled wants; his needs. He said the accident and Lisa's death triggered a breaking point. The suicide attempt was a behavioral symptom representing the break in his organized thought processes. Not knowing the patient that well, and only going by what I shared with him, he reminded me that my job was to help Rex get unstuck and repair the break in his psyche. He used the children's story of Humpy-Dumpty to illustrate his point.

"You're better than all the King's horses and all the King's men" he said. "You can help put that young man back together."

King I thought. *That's Rex*!

From a more clinical perspective, he suggested that I use Acceptance and Commitment Therapy (ACT), which research shows has measureable efficacy in treating PTSD, depression, and anxiety. As I was familiar with ACT, I sometimes thought of it as the therapy *du jour*. I told my colleague that ACT was already in my treatment plan. Yet privately, I was uncertain that Rex's issues could be resolved with any organized or structured approach. There was something missing in Rex's situation, but I could not put my finger on it.

Wednesday, eight p.m. – Wife's Input

That night, I talked to my wife about Rex, but did not provide any identifying information. She has always been very supportive and encouraging. I told her about my theory of survivor's guilt and how he had been diagnosed with PTSD and was taking antidepressants.

"You once told me that the Golden Rule in therapy is Respect; and that respect was really about doing unto others as you would have them do unto you. What you want for your patients you should want for yourself and vice versa" she said warmly.

"I still believe that and use it in my practice. But it's so hard sometimes."

"Sounds like there's more to this though. How are YOU feeling about him and his prognosis?"

"I'm not sure. Up to this point, most of what we cover during our two sessions has been what I consider superficial stuff. I'm hoping for a breakthrough. I'm hoping for a more meaningful exchange between the two of us."

"Maybe it's too early. You always talk about getting people unstuck before they can experience any relief or a breakthrough. Maybe you're the one stuck. I've warned you about burnout. The kind of work you do can be very stressful and sometimes draining."

"You're right about that. Maybe I'm trying too hard or not hard enough. I don't know. I'm seeing him tomorrow for the third session. I'm not sure what to expect."

"You'll cross that bridge when you come to it. It's the uncertainty, I think, that's driving you crazy. We can't always be certain about everything. At the risk of sounding corny, why don't you say your favorite prayer before you go to bed tonight? It may help relieve some of your doubt and maybe open up a new perspective."

She was referring to the Serenity Prayer incorrectly attributed to St. Francis. As an altar boy years ago, I used to say this prayer daily. Believing that prayer is power, I took her advice.

God grant me the Serenity to accept the things I cannot change;
Courage to change the things I can;
And the Wisdom to know the difference.

She was right. Rex is the captain of his own ship. He will steer himself in the direction best for him. I am but an instrument. Like a ship's search light or a beacon on the shore, maybe I could help shed some light onto the dark sea. But are empathy and sympathy enough?

I slept better that night.

Thursday, eight a.m. – Morning Report

At Morning Report, Ramona expressed her surprise at how improved Rex presented. He seemed more lucid and was even conversing with staff and other residents. She said he had made quick progress. He was joking with others and interacting normally. He even asked Ramona "What kind of a guy is Dr. Davila?"

I was flattered and thought that maybe I was partially responsible for his improvement. But Dr. Russell spoke up and said "Yes, I think the effect of the medication is contributing to his early progress. It usually takes longer, but it depends on the individual's metabolism."

I thought *she may be right.* Studies have shown that the combination of talk therapy and medication provide the most promising and efficacious results, above and beyond the administration of a single treatment.

I had quite a few patients to see that day. Due to scheduling issues, my third interview with Rex was not until after lunch.

Thursday, 2:00 p.m. – Third Session

Rex entered my office with a smile. I had never seen this before. He seemed relaxed and comfortable. He sat down and put his hands on my desk.

"What's the agenda today, Doc?"

After the usual small talk; mostly opinions about the facility and his stay here so far, I wanted to dig deeper into his apparent improvement.

"Well, staff tells me that you are doing much better. I'm glad to hear this. To what do you attribute this positive change?"

"I've been thinking less about others and more about me and what I want."

"Really? That's intriguing! Tell me more about that."

His facial expression changed dramatically. He became serious but did not speak for nearly a minute. Then he lowered his head and raised his hands in fists and held them against his eyes and cheeks. He began to quietly sob. The pain he had held inside him began to gush out, exposing his vulnerability for the first time. Emotions he had been so good at holding in now seemed to resist confinement.

"Rex.... Rex.... Rex!" I tried to get his attention. I wanted him to talk. I wanted to know what was going on. Was this some kind of an epiphany? A catharsis?

He began to speak, but he was crying too hard to enunciate. I could barely make out what he wanted to say.

"Rex, talk to me. I can't understand what you're trying to say."

More clearly, he said "I didn't want to get married. I didn't love Lisa. I didn't want to marry Lisa. I wanted out of the marriage."

This was an unexpected confession. My thoughts went back to my colleague's comments. Rex was stuck in a committed relationship. He wanted to get out of the engagement, but didn't know how to do it. The accident and Lisa's tragic death unfortunately became his way out, but it was not what he had planned or hoped for. His confession to me was painfully cathartic. It was a breakthrough.

I allowed Rex to continue talking through his tears. I wanted to give him all the time and space he needed to get through this moment. I gently slid a box of facial tissues in front of him. He pulled out several tissues and wiped his eyes and face. He continued to talk, but more clearly understandable. He was purging the pain, the mental and emotional anguish, the guilt.

He had agreed to marry Lisa because he felt it was the right thing to do "for the family". He felt that his expectations, his wants, his needs were selfish. He decided that it was more important to consider his family and Lisa and the whole "normal thing" to do.

He said that during his short stay here, he saw people who had serious problems; people who had chronic debilitating issues. Their ability to take care of themselves was impaired, and they, therefore, had to depend on others to make decisions for them. He, on the other hand, could make his own decisions and act on them. Up to now, his sense of selfishness had kept him from doing this. He began to realize that he was not being selfish by pursuing his own needs and desires. He realized that unlike the others in the hospital, he was capable of doing this.

He did not blame his family or Lisa.

"This is about me and what I want. But I worry how my family will react to my wanting to be more independent in making my own decisions."

"That's normal. But keep in mind your family made their own choices. You would just be doing the same. Your sister was right about one thing, for your own sake, you will need to move on. But you can only do so in your own way and in your own time."

We went on to discuss ways that he would like to move on. I offered him my full support and encouraged him to trust in his ability to make his own choices along with the expected consequences. He, in turn, acknowledged the challenges ahead of him.

Having said all he wanted to say, Rex stood up and walked to the door to leave. Before exiting, he turned and faced me. "Thanks, Doc. And by the way, I don't want to run a tortilla factory or a bakery."

After the session, I felt good. Rex was making progress. I felt that we had developed a trusting relationship, which helped him to open up to me. He was ashamed of the way he felt, but at the same time he clearly understood how he would proceed from here. I couldn't help but sigh and smile. I entered the details of the session into Rex's computer record.

That night I told my wife all about the third session. As usual, she was very supportive.

"Since he wanted out of the marriage, maybe it was fate or divine intervention that resulted in a way out for the guy" I said.

"So you're saying that the girl's death was divine intervention to help the guy out? That doesn't sound right, my dear. That's awful."

She was right of course. That was not very understanding of me and not what I meant. But the whole thing still bothered and perplexed me. I needed to think only in terms of helping Rex and nothing more. My primary and ethical concern was his welfare.

Friday, eight a.m. – Morning Report

Ramona began by reporting on two new admissions. I noted that I would need to schedule them that day. She then reported that Rex was discharged the previous night.

"Dr. Silva saw the patient and his sister, and they agreed that he was no longer a danger to himself or others. His sister agreed to take responsibility for him. The discharge info is in the patient's computer record. Oh, and, Dr. Davila, Mr. Bonilla left this envelope for you. I didn't open it. Promise!" She giggled as she handed it to me.

I was, naturally, a little disappointed. I had scheduled to see Rex that morning.

Normally, the team – Psychiatrist, Psychologist, Social Worker, Unit Manager, and Charge Nurse – work together when making decisions. But in the absence of the entire team, the Psychiatrist can solely determine discharge criteria.

Rex had been detained for the required 72 hours. The after-hours psychiatrist deemed him fit for discharge.

After Report, I took the envelope with me to my office. I sat at my desk and stared at the unopened white square on my desk. *Should I read it now?*

Then, fearing the worst, I put it in my Daily Planner, thinking *I'll open it later*.

Friday, six p.m. -- Home

When I got home I told my wife about Rex's discharge. She could tell I was disappointed. I felt that I needed more time with him. Unfinished business for me. But maybe for Rex, it was time to move on.

Seeking validation, I said "I feel a little cheated, but I am happy for him. I think we kinda reached a fork in the road. We helped each other. Right?"

She said "Yes; good. I guess the prayer helped. Isn't it Friday, and isn't it time for Happy Hour?" We smiled at each other.

She left for the den and prepared a cocktail for each of us. I turned and opened my Daily Planner to the envelope with the handwritten "Dr. Davila" on it. I took the note card out. It simply read:

Unstuck! Unbroken! Rex

Introduction

We have relations with others. Some are strong ties, others are just so-so. We refer to them as "friends" and relatives, or as "acquaintances", like co-workers whom we like, but do not know so well. "Familiarity breeds contempt" is the old saying. But not always!

Sometimes we connect with people who were acquaintances and who turn out to be friends. Or, in the case of the following story, they turn out to be anything but friendly. There is also a lesson to be learned here. Things and people are not always what they seem. The lesson is: Always be on your guard, and expect the unexpected. Learn to use good judgment and good sense. Be kind, but not vulnerable. Kindness is not a sign of weakness. Beware others may see it as such.

Safety Concerns

"Common sense is not so common."

--- Voltaire (Philosophical Dictionary)

[And let me add: Good sense is needed more than common sense.]

"Better safe than sorry!"

– *Mom*

That morning I opened my email account to find a message from someone with the name of StanMan.... I was not sure if it would be safe to open, but I decided to do just that. The email read: "If your name is Raul Segura, or as we knew you 'Roy', I'm hoping you remember me. I'm Stanley Mandrel, Stan the Man, from St. Bernadette's School for Girls. If this is correct, please reply if you feel okay doing so."

I immediately knew who Stanley Mandrel was. He was a teacher and colleague of mine at St. Bernadette's back in the 70s. Remembering him brought back a lot of memories of my year teaching at this private school in Redemption, a town in upstate New York. It was a parochial school for grade levels 10, 11, and 12. The school had a favorable reputation for education and helping young girls become socially acceptable women. It was a small school with less than 100 girls, who were mostly from surrounding small towns. I knew little about the school when I first agreed to teach social studies there. However, once I began, I realized how different my view of women was from that of the administration. This was 1977, but it might as well have been 1877.

The administration was not so much misogynistic, as much as it heavily relied on Old Testament attitudes towards women. The girls were told that someday they would make great mothers and wives to their providers, namely their husbands. They were taught that all they needed to learn was how to be happy "housewives" and pure of heart in God's eyes. Life's fulfillment, they were told, is in restraint and obedience. They would become paragons of womanhood. There was little room for anything else. What else could there be for these future 'homemakers'?

After one year, I made it clear to the administration that I could not be an accomplice to this "brainwashing." They did not appreciate my announcement and were more than happy to send me on my way, never to return.

I became friends with Stanley, who taught history. His attitude toward women was similar to that of the school administration. But we found other things in common, so I avoided the topic all together. We talked sports and academia, and the fact that we were both altar boys when we were of age. Politics was a little contentious, but it never divided us. He did not think women should be in politics or in business ventures. I identified more with being a "feminist."

So naturally, I was hesitant to respond to his email. Nevertheless, later that day I replied that of course I remembered him. I gave him my number and let him know a good time to call. He did.

We talked about our teaching experiences at the school and why we both left there. Stanley took a job as a history teacher at a large high school in New York City. He loved his job. I told him I had gone on to teach college-level Psychology, married, had two daughters, and was now divorced. He had married twice and divorced twice, but had no children.

Eventually, the conversation turned to us getting together. But he was in NYC, and I was in Houston. He told me that every other year he would travel to Mexico. He said he really enjoyed going there, especially to see the ruins in the Yucatan and then travel by bus to

Mexico City. He sounded very excited about those trips and said he was planning another one for that summer.

"How would you feel about going along with me? I think you'd like it."

"Well, I don't know. I'd have to think about it. I've heard it's not very safe for tourists."

"Nonsense! That's just the media always trying to portray Mexico in a negative way. I have never had a problem. It's perfectly safe where I go. You just have to avoid certain places; just like you have to do here. There are places right here in New York City that I stay away from."

"Well, maybe you're right. But I still need to think about it."

"No problem. I'll give you a few weeks and then call you. I hope you decide to go. You won't regret it."

Two weeks later, Stanley called me back. We discussed a few details, including the approximate cost, and I told him that it was doable. He said he would make all the arrangements. He would fly from New York and I from Houston, and we'd rendezvous in Merida, Mexico. The more he talked about it, the more I felt comfortable in my decision to take some time off for myself.

I told Stan "I spoke to my girls and they were okay with the idea. Even my ex-wife was in favor of a vacation from school."

"Your ex-wife? Really, Raul...I mean Roy? Well I can see who wore the pants in that marriage."

I pretended I did not hear what he said. Ignoring him in this regard was my best option.

"I'll send you the paperwork and information by email once it's confirmed. I'll keep our budget within reason. I'm not rich or cheap. But I am frugal." We both laughed.

I was looking forward to the trip, so on the designated day I was willing and ready. My flight was nonstop from Houston. When I arrived at the airport terminal in Merida, Stanley was there to greet me. I couldn't miss him. He stood over six feet tall; and he had not changed much since I last saw him over 20 years earlier. We made our way to the hotel. He was pleased that my Spanish was passable, although he said that he never had any problem getting around speaking only English.

The hotel was beautiful and accommodating. Stanley reserved one room with two double beds. We had dinner in the hotel and then agreed to have breakfast no later than 8:00 a.m., giving us ample time to be ready for the tour to the pyramids -- Chitchen Itza and Tulum.

That night, as we lay in bed, lights out, Stan began a conversation with me.

"Why did you get divorced? And with two kids, at that?"

"Oh, we had our differences. It was not an easy decision. She met a guy at her work and a relationship developed. It eventually became intimate. I was angry and disheartened. We both saw separation as our best and only option. And you?"

"Marriage and divorce are natural progressions. Like life and death. One is the beginning and the other is the end."

"Yeah" I said. "But life and death is a onetime thing; marriage and divorce are repeatable. You married twice and divorced twice. So, do you plan to marry again?"

"Sure! Most likely! Divorce doesn't agree with me. Remember the old saying 'You can't live with them; and you can't live without them'. But I don't want any children."

I laughed. "You're something else, Stan!" He continued to ramble for I don't know how long. I fell asleep not knowing what other pearls of wisdom he wanted to share with me.

After breakfast, the tour bus picked us up on schedule. The drive was only an hour and a half from Merida. After arriving, Stanley immediately urged me to climb to the top of Chichen Itza with him. I did. It was exhilarating, but exhausting. By the time we got to the top, I was spent and had to take time to catch my breath. My heart was pumping, but I felt good...even healthy.

"You out of shape, young man?" Stanley asked. I just laughed and nodded my head.

I slowly walked around the top of the pyramid viewing the unbelievable panorama for as far as the eye could see. It was, indeed, breathtaking. Eventually I made my way to the edge of one side. I've always known that I had a fear of falling, which is different from fear of heights. So when I got too close to the ledge, I froze for just a few seconds until I could get my bearings.

It was at that moment that I sensed someone close behind me. It startled me, and I quickly turned around. Stanley was standing directly behind me with his arms extended toward me, palms open, as if he were leaning them up against a wall. I immediately and swiftly moved passed him. *Was he reaching out to push me?* I wondered.

"You scared the crap out of me, Stan" I gasped.

"Sorry. I noticed that the wind was blowing really hard and I became concerned for your safety. I just wanted to grab you in case you fell forward. You seemed a little unsteady."

"Thanks! I guess! I'm fine."

He added "You know a woman fell to her death here a few years ago. It was an accident, but authorities were suspicious that someone might have pushed her. Really scary...and sad."

"Thanks for telling me. I'll be more careful" I muttered.

We climbed down from Chichen Itza, slowly. The tour guide met us and after about an hour led us back to the bus for our trip to Tulum.

After arriving at Tulum, which is smaller than and not as high as Chichen Itza, I was undecided as to whether to climb it or not. With Stanley's suggestion that I not look over the edge, I went up again. This time, I avoided turning my back on Stanley. He made me feel nervous after the incident at Chichen Itza. The view of the Caribbean Sea was magnificent. The climb and the descent went well.

We had an outdoor lunch buffet and enjoyed the rest of the afternoon. Our tour guide explained that the Yucatan pyramids are not as old as the Egyptian ones. The Mexican pyramids of Quintana Roo were built about 1000 B.C., while the Egyptian pyramids were built around 2700 B.C. After lunch, we headed back to Merida and our hotel. Stanley and I had dinner at a nearby restaurant. Later we had drinks. The evening was pleasant, and we enjoyed each other's company.

The next morning, we traveled by bus to Campeche, a fishing village. We visited the cathedral and main plaza. Campeche is serene, tranquil and quite a change from the crowds and activity at Chichen Itza and Tulum. I liked it there, and someday I hope to return.

We spent the night in Campeche and the next morning headed by bus to Mexico City. Stanley did not speak to me during the entire ride. He had become sullen, brooding. I felt that he believed I distrusted him. There was an unexpected tension between us. We arrived at the bus depot in Mexico City late, around 11:00 p.m. Once we got our bags, Stanley began walking alone ahead of me.

"Stanley" I yelled. "Aren't we going to the hotel?" Without turning toward me he answered "We are. We're walking. It's really close. I told you I've been here many times and I know this area. It's not far. And it's perfectly safe."

I did not feel safe. We walked down several streets; turning here and turning there. It was dark and very few street lights, no people and no activity. I felt like we were going around in circles.

"Why don't we just get a taxi?" I said with some desperation in my voice.

He seemed agitated and snapped "I told you, I know this area. The hotel is close. Just follow me." He then turned to his right, into what looked to me like an alley way. There was an ominous darkness about that abandoned path.

"Don't you trust me? Come on! Follow me! We're almost there." He headed into the alley. I felt tense, anxious. It was true. I didn't trust him at that point. My anxiety was building.

Then suddenly, a taxi, with bright lights came toward me. I flagged it down. The driver stopped. I asked "Do you know where the Melia Hotel is near here?"

In Spanish he answered "Sure! Hop in. It's just down the street."

I called out to Stanley "Hey, Stan. This taxi will take us to the hotel. Come on. Get in."

He reluctantly walked back toward me. I could sense that he was angry at me for not trusting him and for not staying with his plan to walk to the hotel. I'll never forget the look on his face. Ghastly! He got into the front passenger seat of the taxi and slammed the door shut.

"Senor, please!" the taxi driver said in Spanish. "Careful with my door!"

I sat in the back seat. I could feel Stan's anger. He had become frustrated. And in my opinion, for no apparent reason other than I wouldn't follow his directives. I realized that things needed to change before the situation between us would worsen.

When we checked into the hotel, I asked to switch the reservation from one room with two beds to two single rooms.

I informed Stan "I'm really tired and want to rest quietly alone tonight if you don't mind."

"No. Not at all. I'm okay with that. I'm a little tired too. I'll see you in the morning for breakfast." He turned and walked to the bar.

I went to my room and felt relieved. I no longer felt safe around Stanley. I don't know why, but his demeanor had changed since that day atop Chichen Itza.

I called my daughters to let them know that I was okay and that the trip was going smoothly. This was, of course, a lie. But I felt much better after talking to them. And, I was glad I got to sleep alone and not in the same room with Stanley.

The next morning, we met for breakfast and continued with our plan to visit the churches and a museum, and then have a late lunch in the main Zocalo. We had a very pleasant and satisfying morning. After lunch, we casually strolled back to the hotel for an afternoon siesta.

As we entered the lobby area, we were met by several uniformed police and two men dressed in suits who approached us. They focused on Stanley.

"Are you Senor Stanley Mandrel?" one of the suited men asked.

"Yes." Stan hesitantly replied.

"Come with us, senor." They took him by the arms and put handcuffs on him. A police officer on each side of him, they led him out of the hotel. One of the suited men turned to me.

"And your name, senor? And your passport." I told him my name and handed him my passport which I always carry with me when out of the country.

"Senor Segura, are you traveling with Senor Mandrel?"

"Well, yes I am."

"Then you will need to come with us also. We just have a few questions to ask you."

I was shaking in my shoes. *What was this all about? What had Stanley done? Why am I being detained?*

They led us outside to two waiting police cars. They took Stan in one and me in the other. When we arrived at the Estacion de Policia, Stan was taken to one room and I to another. One of the suited men asked me how I knew Stan. I told him the whole story of Stan and I reuniting after 20 plus years. He asked if I was aware that Mr. Mandrel was wanted for the murders of several people over the past eight years, including the murder of a woman who was pushed off the top of Chichen Itza. He said that Stan had been on their radar for many years, but they only now had enough evidence to charge him for at least four murders. *Was Stan a serial killer?*

"Are you sure Stan killed someone?" I asked.

"Not killed, senor; murdered. In some instances it is legal to kill. Murder is illegal. In Mexico, you can only be charged with murder; not with killing someone."

I did remember reading somewhere that when the Bible was first translated into English the 6th commandment was "Thou shalt not kill." But in some later versions of the commandment, it was changed to "Thou shalt not murder." Why? Because there are many ways we can kill other humans legally and with impunity: such as war, execution, self-defense.

"What's going to happen to him" I asked. I had become aware of the seriousness of the situation. Scared, I was standing on a psychological ledge.

"Well, he will go to trial, of course. In Mexico, a suspect is presumed guilty until proven innocent. He will have his opportunity in court to prove his innocence."

"I'd like to see him...to talk to him."

"That is not permitted, senor. I will have someone take you back to your hotel now."

After one hour, the detective let me go and a police woman drove me back to the hotel. I thought *Stan wouldn't appreciate a police woman in charge of him!*

Once back at the hotel, I felt safe and out of danger, but a little confused. I thought I knew Stan, but I surmised that I didn't. No longer having to concern myself with Stanley's attitude and suspicious nature, I relaxed; glad that I went with my instincts, my gut feelings. I didn't want to believe it, but Stan was a dangerous man.

I did not leave the hotel that night. I ate dinner and then had a few drinks in the hotel bar. The bartender was a female. Again I thought *Stan wouldn't like having a female bartender*. I don't know why I was thinking about Stan. He was out of my life. I was no longer concerned about my safety. Still, the past few days were a lot to digest. I thought of my daughters.

The next morning, after a satisfying breakfast, the shuttle took me to the airport. Part of me wanted to stay longer in Mexico City, but also a part of me wanted to leave...leave Stan behind. I boarded the plane and took a seat next to a lovely middle-aged woman.

Before takeoff, we started a conversation. "How was your trip to Mexico?" she asked.

"It was nice. I liked it more than I anticipated. We started out at the pyramids in the Yucatan and then ended up in Mexico City. Not knowing the country and it being my first time, I admit I was a little worried about my safety."

"We?" she asked.

"Oh, I was with an old friend. He had to stay behind. Long story!"

"You didn't feel safe in Mexico?"

"Oh, yes I did. But not at first. I guess the stories of drugs and violence on the news got to me."

"I see, but surely you understand that America is a lot more dangerous than Mexico. In fact, it is more dangerous than most countries. We have the highest murder rate in the world. Some places are safer than others, but you have to be familiar with them. I live in Houston and my sister lives in San Antonio, and we both sometimes feel unsafe in certain parts of town."

"You're right. I live in Houston, too. I feel pretty safe there. I've never had any problems. But this was my first and only trip to Mexico. You can understand my uneasiness."

"Oh, of course I do. But I come to Mexico often because I have relatives here. I stay with them, and I always feel safe. I've never had a problem." She smiled exposing one gold tooth.

"I'm glad to hear that."

After takeoff, I was a little tired so I closed my eyes to get in a brief siesta. I seemed to keep going in and out of sleep. I began to experience what seemed like hallucinations. I was between awake and asleep states, or half awake and half asleep, or in an early stage of sleep.

Specifically, I could hear Stanley's voice in the seat behind me talking to someone next to him. Eventually, I could visualize him talking to a strange woman. *Was she the one who fell from the pyramid and died?* He was saying "You know I've been to Mexico so many times, I can get around almost anywhere without any help. I can walk blindfolded or in the dark to the same hotels I always use. I know the streets of Mexico like the back of my hand. And I travel alone. No distractions!"

The woman asked "Aren't you afraid to be walking the streets at night alone?"

"Oh, no." Stan answered. "It's perfectly safe. Nothing to worry about!"

At that very moment, the plane jerked and thumped and brought me into awareness. I sat up in my seat. Of course the voice and image weren't really Stan. It was a hallucination.

A soft bell sounded, and the "Fasten Seat Belts" light came on.

The captain came on the PA system: "We've encountered a little turbulence there, folks. Nothing serious. I'm going to adjust our altitude, and it should be smooth sailing after that. Until then, stay seated and keep your seat belts on until the seat belt light is turned off. Thank you!"

Finally, the realization hit me: I could have been one of Stanley's victims. I relaxed knowing that I had dodged a bullet. Was it common sense or intuition that got me through this? Or was it plain old-fashioned good sense that guided me? Was it also my instincts and gut feelings that saved me? I don't know. I just know that I'm on a plane now going home ... alive and safe.

"Are you married?" the woman next to me asked.

"Divorced" I said. "I have two daughters."

"That's sweet. I'm also divorced. I kinda like being single" she smiled.

"Oh? You don't want to remarry?" I asked.

"Maybe, if the right man comes along. I'm game. And you?"

I sensed a connection with this woman. I sensed possibilities with her.

"What is your name, curious lady?"

"I'm Irma."

"Irma, my name is Raul. But people call me Roy."

"Humm! Which name do you prefer?"

"No one has ever asked me that. I guess Raul. And to answer your question: Yes. I'm game. I'd remarry if the right woman comes along." Yes. There were definite possibilities here.

Once the fasten seatbelt's light turned off, I excused myself and walked back to the WC. Once alone in the private little lavatory, my mind began to clear. The plane shook and felt unsteady. Turbulence always scares me. And yet, I felt safe on this jumbo 747.

Wide awake now, I had a disturbing thought:

Is anyone...anywhere...ever...really...perfectly...safe?

[*Note: In 2007, the UNESCO World Heritage named the Mexican Pyramids of the Yucatan one of the Seven Wonders of the World. Also, as a consequence of years of damage by tourists, and for their safety, in 2008, the Mexican government banned all tourists/visitors from climbing the pyramids.]*

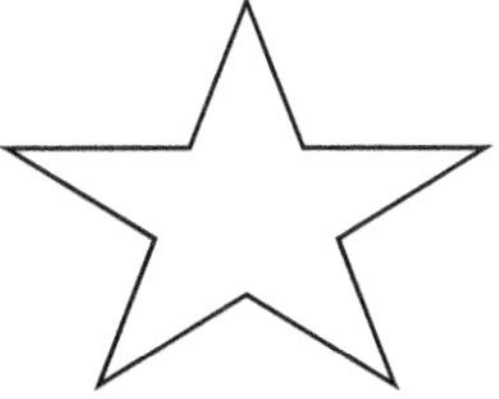

Introduction

How strong is your faith? Your hope? Your love? These questions are often difficult to answer. They are also difficult to ask. If someone believes that God is good, then why is there so much bad in the world, and always has been. The story of Adam and Eve tells us that there was "bad" even within the first family. Perhaps good and bad are at opposite ends of a continuum. Perhaps both are the destiny of humankind.

I interviewed the man in this next story. He shared with me his journey of faith, hope, and love. He also told me he was "bad". His behavior defined his attitude. Regardless of what he believed, or wants others to believe, his behavior is what mattered in the end. He saw his behaviors as good deeds. And we all know about good deeds: (as mentioned earlier) They do not go unpunished!

A Religious Guy

"If God didn't exist, Man would have to invent Him". -
Voltaire

"He's just a sensitive and very religious boy" my mother would tell family, friends and neighbors. I hated it when she said that. People always agreed.

"Yes. He not only acts saintly, he has that saintly look. All that's missing is the little halo. Where did he get that quality?" they would ask.

"Who knows? He's a very devoted Christian boy. I guess God just made him that way. So cute!" my mother would reply.

I never liked being called 'sensitive' or 'religious' or saintly'; and I liked it less after I turned 30 years old. Men over 30 are not "sensitive", nor are they "cute". They may be a lot of things, but in the Latino culture, 30 year old men are not "sensitive". I don't mean to stereotype... Okay, maybe a little, and I know it's wrong to do that.

However, I did, and I do, identify with the moniker 'religious'. I was an altar boy and attended church daily; even did volunteer work for the church and school. Prayers before meals, morning and night prayers were routine. I wanted so badly to please God! Still do!

In any case, truth be known, maybe I am kinda sensitive ...but only about a few things. I like dogs, especially friendly, playful dogs and puppies. I like puppies. I don't have a dog, but I had one when I was a kid. She was a loving dog to me, but she liked to bite strangers who got too close to me. After a few incidents, they -- the people at Animal Control -- came and got her and 'put her down'. I cried for days, couldn't eat, sleep, or take interest in school. My family and friends were of little consolation. They were, nevertheless, understanding (because I was a sensitive boy), for about a week.

I'm also sensitive to sad movies and music. As a child, I would always cry when watching a sad movie. Something about the suffering of others impacted me. I like all kinds of music. Music moves me, emotionally. It's my therapy. If music doesn't impact me emotionally, aesthetically, then I don't care for it. Over the years, I've collected vinyl records and CDs. More recently, I just download music to my PC and smart phone. Music removes me from all unpleasant 'here and now' situations. Even with background music, I feel more relaxed, mellow, and able to cope and think better. I used to play piano as a kid, but I lost that skill years ago. I had and have no skill for it. I admire people who can play musical instruments. I actually envy them. Musical acuity is a talent, an art, a gift. It's magical!

Relevant to my religious sensitivity, I have a platonic love for my fellow man. Call it *agape*. And yet despite my love for mankind in general, I don't like certain (kinds of) people, and I'm not very sensitive to them. Some people can be jerks. They can be uncompromising and selfish. They can be liars, hypocrites, manipulators, phonies, fakes, frauds. I could go on about this, but I think I've made my point. People can't be trusted! In a movie I once watched, the father tells his son something to the effect "don't have any positive expectations of people ... They'll always let you down, and you'll always be disappointed." The father was referring to his wife, the boy's mother, who was divorcing the boy's father.

Some people get on my nerves. They frustrate me. Many people can't drive, but they have licenses. Many people don't speak properly or grammatically correct. They can't read or spell words common in the English language. Sentence construction is a lost form of communication. This is one reason some people get on my nerves, big time. I'm told I should be more tolerant, more understanding and patient; that I should accept various American dialects. Why?

I'm married. My wife tells people that she married me because I'm a sensitive and religious guy, and "you just can't find a good, sensitive man nowadays." Well, I'm happily married, but I still don't like it when she says that to people. One reason I married her, aside from the physical attraction, was that she has always been patient with and understanding of me. Patience is a virtue, and I need people to be patient and understanding with me. She pays attention to me. I hate it when people don't pay attention to me or ignore me. Mostly, I just want modest attention, recognition, and acknowledgement. I've earned it! I deserve it. Is that asking too much?

Most people are not patient. They want immediate everything: immediate satisfaction, gratification, attention. "I want it (all) now!" And "I want more!"

People are greedy and selfish all over the world. But as far as I know, we are the only country that actually has an ongoing TV show entitled "American Greed," Am I being too judgmental? Cynical? Too critical? Or am I just being realistic? Am I hypocritical because I demand that others be patient and understanding while I am not? Maybe!

*****

The reader is probably wondering where I'm going with what sounds like a radio talk-show host rant. Okay, I'll tell you the truth. As I write this account, I'm sitting in a state prison, behind bars. I was charged with capital murder. I killed a man. And I did it for his own good!

I worked for a printing company for about 8 years. I got along with most of my coworkers, except for one.

On the surface, Norman was a nice guy. But he often wanted to talk about religion, usually about its destructiveness, a very sensitive subject for me. I tried to avoid the topic, but he persisted in bringing it up every time we had lunch together at a nearby family diner. We would sit in a booth and start off talking about work-related issues. Then the subject would turn to any current news – usually bad news. There is always plenty of bad news.

One day, he started with: "So, I saw on TV last night that some deranged maniac, a kid with an assault rifle, went and shot up a school and killed and wounded innocent children and a few teachers. Where was your God during that disaster? If He is responsible for all that is good in the world, then He should be just as responsible for all the bad that happens. Right?"

Norman proclaimed long ago that he was not only an atheist, but an agnostic atheist. He did not believe in God or in any Deity, and said that no one could provide any hard evidence that such a being ever existed. He knew this was a touchy issue to me, but he felt that I needed to accept his way (the logical, rational way) of thinking. He wanted me to understand why believing in an unverifiable, supreme entity was simply mindless, unproven, unfounded, and without merit.

It would be an understatement to say that I don't like Atheists. When in 1995, a leader of the Atheist Movement in Texas was killed, along with her son and adopted daughter, I was actually pleased to learn about it. I thought *that's what they get for not believing in God and for pontificating the absurdity of the very existence of God.*

For a couple of years, almost daily, I felt compelled to listen to Norman's ranting, not only about his disbelief in God, but also about the foolishness of people who base their life decisions on their faith and religion, and not on reason and fact. He believed that the people who wrote and live by the Bible – Old and New Testaments -- and the Koran, or any other holy book, were delusional extremists who didn't want to take responsibility for their own actions and thus attributed everything to a higher power, which they must adore, obey, and fear. He even "attacked" Jesus.

"The Bible was written by men and the New Testament was written all about Jesus. Everybody wrote about Jesus, except Jesus himself! He never wrote a thing. If what he said and did was so important, why didn't Jesus write about it himself? Was he illiterate?"

Now, I was really getting hot under the collar. He went on to insist that there was no evidence, proof, or scientific basis for the existence of an omnipotent or any God-like being. He saw religion as "a distorted, alternate reality." He did concede that the man Jesus existed.

Admittedly, his arguments were often more convincing than mine, because I expressed that my love of God and trust in God is based on Faith. And Faith can "move mountains." He would laugh: "Have you moved any mountains lately?"

One day, I said "AbNorman (my nickname for him), even our money says 'In God we trust". He laughed again, out loud! Now he was really getting under my skin. My faith and America's trust in God had become a joke to him. However, he insisted he was not cynical.

"Look" he said. "The reason that phrase is on our money is because it is 'in our money we trust'. The almighty dollar is more important than your almighty God!"

"In the justice system, we are asked to put our right hand on a bible and swear to tell the whole truth and nothing but the truth – 'so help me God'. Is that not a fact?" I asked.

He opined "It's a fact that many people lie under oath. Look, my friend, religion is just a way that the rich and powerful keep the poor under their control, keep them down. That's why so many people believe that if you are rich, it's a sign of God's blessing; the wealthy are blessed by God with money and brains. Hallelujah! The more money you have, the more blessed you are by God. We poor schmucks are not as blessed, or loved as much by your alleged God.

"No, my friend, you cannot substitute religion for reality, nor faith for practicality. Face reality, and you will deface God! Know ye the Truth and not the Myth, and ye shall be set free. And the rich, like some politicians, go along window-dressing and feigning to be religious in order to give the illusion that God is on their side. They use their religion and their belief in God as a weapon and as a vote-getter. I call them 'CHINOs': Christians In Name Only. I feel sorry for people whose heads are in a cloud of religion. I believe in facts, evidence, and proof. That's all that really matters in this materialistic world. I admit that I don't believe in God, but I also admit that I can't prove that he doesn't exist. So, the existence of God is a moot point! And by the way, the existence of Satan is also unproven, yet popular.

"And furthermore" he continued, "we are a so-called Christian nation yet we put Greed above Good. We are obsessed with wealth and ownership and war. Even the taking of land that we wanted was justified by Manifest Destiny – God's will. Might makes right. We will kill someone who tries to steal our car battery. Yes, a battery is more important than a life. The mighty gun is our staff and our rod. Religion has caused more death and destruction and division than even Satan could have imagined. Evil delights in the havoc religion leaves in its wake.

"And what's more, why are there so many religions? Catholic, Protestant – there are a lot of those – Judaism and Islam. Every group or organization which believes in God has its own God. Yet you all preach that there is only One True God. It just doesn't make any sense. God exists only in your mind and in the minds of those who are self-righteous and holier-than-thou radicals. False prophets trump their non-existent gods. Hypocrites, one and all!"

"So you believe in Satan, but not God?" I interjected. "Your negativity must be oppressive. You are a miserable and sad person if you have no God, and only Satan."

"The facts and reality support the notion that there is evil in the world. For lack of a better explanation, let's just call it the work of evil people. Likewise, good is simply the work of good folk."

And so it went during our daily lunches. But then, there came a day when I felt I needed to take this issue to another, perhaps final, step. I asked Norman what it would take to convince him that God or Allah or any other deity really does exist, not just in our minds and hearts, but in "reality". Norman paused and then responded.

"That's simple. If I could see God, or any so-called deity, face-to-face and have him or her -- I've heard that God could be a woman -- look directly at me, eye to eye! If I could see your God face-to-face, in the flesh, then maybe I could accept that God in reality does exist. Introduce me to God. Take me to Him. Have him prove to me that he is God! It's that simple!"

I went home that day thinking hard on what Norman had said to me at lunch. I examined my emotional attitude first, because I was sensitive to what he had expressed to me. Then I thought about it as rational and realistic as I could. Lastly, I turned to my faith in deciding if and how I should act. Faith and hope is not a plan. Yet my faith would lead me to do good and not harm. I prayed for guidance from God. I asked for courage, strength, and commitment. I begged for a resolve in my vexation.

The next morning, I dressed for work and put my .38-caliber handgun into my fanny pack, the one with the American flag design. I made sure it was loaded and easily accessible. Feeling confident, I went to work as usual. I did not mention this to my wife.

At lunch time, Norman and I walked over to the diner and sat in our usual booth. We talked about work and other mundane stuff. After we finished lunch and we were about to leave, it was I who brought up the subject of God.

"AbNorman, I've been thinking about what you said yesterday when I asked you what would convince you of God's existence. You said that if you could have a physical face-to-face meeting with God, you might then believe He really does exist. I've taken that to heart. I've prayed about it, and I think I can help you come to believe in God. I want you to meet God, in person, face-to-face." I paused at his perplexed look.

Feeling the most anxiety I have ever felt in my life, I eked out the words "I think I can help you."

Having said that, I brought the .38-calliber handgun out from my fanny pack, aimed it at Norman, and shot him directly in the chest. His face was startled but blank and frozen in time. Then his body slowly slouched down to his left and rested on the booth seat, his head just under the bright sun shining through the window. He was dead.

Of course there was a big commotion in the restaurant; people running, women screaming, a lot of panic in the air. Some people called 911. I don't remember much after that. When I was able to get my thoughts together, I set the pistol on the table and waited. The police arrived; grabbed me, handcuffs and the whole "take him in, arrest him" thing.

Held in jail for about 4 weeks, I awaited my trial. No bond was posted. My wife visited me and was sorrowful, tearful. To her, what I had done was incredulous.

"Why? What possessed you?"

I thought of an old movie title, and I replied "They shoot horses, don't they?"

She didn't know what else to say. She cried. I cried for her.

The trial was quick. A bench trial; no jury. "Do you swear to tell the truth, the whole truth and nothing but the truth?" I pled guilty. When I was asked why I shot AbNorman, I said something to the effect: "He said that he would believe in God only if he were to meet God face-to-face, so I did him a favor and dispatched him to meet God, so that he might believe. I'm convinced that he believes now. I believe that he has had a "come to Jesus" experience. I'm sure he believes in God now! I did the right thing. It was for his benefit." The judge pronounced my sentence without prejudice.

In the eyes of the law, I had no defense. My fate was in the hands of the true Judge – God. Despite my defense attorney's arguments and objections, I was sentenced to life without the possibility of parole. The judge ended by saying "May God have mercy on you!"

*****

So, here I sit in prison still waiting on God's mercy. I guess I should just be thankful that I'm alive, that I have a place to sleep, three meals a day, something resembling health care, and some minor liberties. I'm okay!

After living with prison inmates for a number of months, I began to learn about the prison culture and lifestyles. I discovered that many inmates "find religion," find God while in prison. Some reasons are obvious: isolation, lack of stimulation, a reflection on their crime(s), an acknowledgment of their "conscience", guilt, and a new-found faith in a higher power.

I arrived with all that. I didn't need to "turn to religion". God was already real in my life. Still, there was something troubling me. I didn't quite feel at peace. It wasn't guilt that I felt. Many inmates I met did not feel guilty about their crimes, or about the people they hurt, the lives they destroyed. Most of them had only one regret: getting caught! They all thought they could get away with their crimes. I did not feel that way. I acknowledged what I did and accepted responsibility for it. I had God. God was on my side. Prison is just a man-made system, an invention of convenience.

I also learned that many state correctional systems have attempted to provide a two-fold approach to incarceration: punishment and rehabilitation. The warden and the guards support the punitive part of this dichotomy, and auxiliary staff provides the rehab part in the form of therapies and sports and authorized "entertainment", such as movies and table games. Staff is also involved in other activities such as prison work and education programs (which I took advantage of), visitation privileges from family and friends, and other off prison ground work, such as road crews, and volunteerism. I started doing research in the make-shift library, which had access to the internet. This was closely monitored by the guards. I wanted to learn more about prison culture.

It was part of the rehabilitation or treatment program (usually opposed by the guards) to provide and make available psychological services. One of the concerns guiding the decision to have psychological services was suicide. Searching the internet, I learned that suicides occur more often in certain occupations. The ten professions with suicide rates in highest to lowest order are:

Doctors, Dentists, Police Officers (including Prison Guards), Veterinarians, financial services, real estate agents, electricians, lawyers, farmers, and pharmacists.*

*****

Eventually, as expected, I was called to meet and speak to an assigned psychologist, a Dr. Mendez. He was about 50ish, a short, stocky man, with a kind face and piercing eyes. His voice was gentle, caring, clear and crisp. He seemed to genuinely care about his patients.

"Have a seat, young man. What is your number? And what is your name and date of birth?

"You have all that stuff, Doc."

"Yes, but I need to verify it with you...to make sure I have the right person."

I gave him the information. What could I possibly tell this man? How could he be of any help to me? I've always thought of psychology as a secular profession; lacking in spiritual considerations. After all, Sigmund Freud was an atheist. [Later I would learn that there is a branch of therapy called Pastoral Counseling, which takes into consideration the religious beliefs and practices of the client/patient. I like that.] Nevertheless, I thought it might be a good idea to give this psychologist a chance, and to see what might evolve from this and future meetings.

"You're not a psychiatrist, are you?" I asked.

“No. A psychiatrist is a medical doctor who specializes in psychiatry, a branch of medicine that combines psychology and medication”.

“So I can’t get any drugs from you? Not that I want or need any.”

“I can recommend medication to the MD, if I determine you need it; if the symptoms meet criteria for a specific diagnosis.”

“I’m not crazy, doc. I killed a man and sent him to his Maker. The way I see it, I did him a favor. He’s in a better place now. He didn’t believe in God, and now he does. I’m sure of it. I know that in God’s eyes, I did the right thing.”

“I see. Okay, tell me about yourself; tell me your story, beginning from as far back as you care to remember.”

For whatever reason, I was ready and willing to open up to this man. It was as if no one had ever cared about how I felt, what I believed, what I had to say – until now. My wife cared, but she wouldn’t be of much help to me now. So, this doctor wanted me to tell him my life story, in my own words, from my own perspective. And so I told him as much as I could during that first session. In the sessions that followed, I continued to open up about everything that mattered to me: my childhood, my parents, my wife and marriage, my schooling, my achievements and my failures, my joys and my disappointments, my anger, and my love of God.

Dr. Mendez listened carefully and patiently, sometimes writing things down on an OfficeMax pad. He always looked right into my eyes when I spoke. He focused on me and only me. I was the center of his attention. I felt uplifted when talking to him. I also felt like a burden was slowly being lifted; a burden that I had been aware of, but could not identify.

"So, do you have any regrets or remorse surrounding your crime? Your offense?"

"The only regret I have is the effect all this has had on my wife and kids, and parents. Because of my actions, they have gone through a lot of pain and suffering. My mom used to say that I was a sensitive boy, a religious boy. But look at what I did and what I have caused!"

"I see. Your mom was right. You are a sensitive person after all. And obviously a religious person. But what about the family and friends of the man you killed?"

I could not stop my eyes from swelling, nor the tears from escaping. "I never wanted to hurt anyone. I meant what I did to be a good thing. I know right from wrong. I'm not a bad person. I'm spiritual, and I only want things to be good, positive, Godly. I hope they don't hate me."

"You hope who doesn't hate you?"

"My wife and parents; and, yes, his family, AbNorman's family, and his friends also. My family means so much to me. They've always been good to me. They should not have to suffer because of my actions. Could you talk to them?"

"Whatever they need to be told should come from you. I'm sure they don't hate you. Do you hate yourself?"

"A little, I guess."

"If you believe that God loves you, you have no reason not to love yourself. I can't talk to the families unless they ask to speak to me. And, I cannot share what you and I have talked about. Confidentiality is imperative. It was on the agreement form you signed earlier. We have a trusting relationship, and what you say in here to me is private and only between the two of us."

"What about the stuff you write in your notes?"

"Those are private, general statements for documentation purposes only; no specifics or details. I assure you."

After several months of these weekly sessions, I believed Dr. Mendez to be both patient and understanding. One day, I asked "Okay. So what's your diagnosis of me? And is there a "prognosis" for me?"

Dr. Mendez sat back in his chair and put his hands together as if he were praying. "This is what I think. You are not mentally ill. You do not meet criteria for a major disorder or diagnosis. You do not need medication. The prognosis is good, but only if you are willing to do something. You must take your faith and direct it toward a positive goal. Killing a man was a negative intent, a negative goal, no matter how you rationalize it to have been with good intentions. This is something you must accept and incorporate into future behaviors."

"I'm not sure I understand. Like, how can I do that?"

"The first thing you must do is ask God for forgiveness. And He will forgive you if you do something that resembles atonement."

"And how can I do that? I'm already in prison."

"Incarceration is not atonement. Studies have shown that 'imagination' is a good emotional release. Imagination replaces reality; kind of like the way religion sometimes replaces reality. Imagination helps release the anger. It's a coping mechanism. Inmates at another prison were surveyed and asked if they could use their imagination to create a different scenario of the crime incident; imagining what they could have done differently. Did they consider the consequences, and did they imagine how they would feel afterwards?

"The results of the survey suggested that over 90% of the inmates answered 'No' to both questions. They said 'I didn't think much about it. I just did it'. Or 'I really didn't care one way or the other. There was a lot of stuff going on in my life.' Or, 'I had a plan, but you do what you gotta do. Imaginin' it aint the same as doin' it. So I did it.' And 'I can't imagine it differently than what it was.' Unable to free their attitude or just imagine a different scenario, they had no choice but to act on their feelings; often negative feelings and thoughts.

"So, I have an idea for you to use your religion as imagination. This may be a step toward atonement. I suggest we get authorization from the warden for you to start a faith-based group. If permitted, network with inmates who are interested in such a group and plan weekly meetings. You can structure it any way you want. Your goal should be to help inmates find faith in God and/or strengthen their existing faith. You can have a positive impact on those who are struggling with their faith in God. Imagine that you can introduce them to God without killing them. You might even be able to help those who have agnostic leanings. You can do a lot in prison. You have more freedom to do good than you think."

I left his office feeling "reborn". I was given a second chance to please God. The next day, I wrote a formal letter to the Warden requesting permission to start a faith-based group. I detailed some of the preliminary plans and formation. A week later, the warden sent me an Authorization letter. He required that I submit a weekly report detailing the group meetings. He wanted names of participants, topics covered, and a summary of each group meeting.

At the first group meeting, there were 12 participants. *Like the 12 apostles*, I thought. On the first day of the group, one of the inmates asked "Do you know God?" I was taken aback by this unexpected question. I thought for a moment and then replied.

"I deeply *believe* in God, but I'd have to say I don't *know* God. I hope to know God after I die. Does that answer your question?" My response actually helped me to better understand my relationship with God and my attitude toward Him. Knowing is not the same as believing.

The inmate smiled. "Yes. I believe in God and I also hope to know Him someday."

Our group continued to meet once a week in an assigned area. As of today, there are about 15-20 participants. I am so very satisfied, knowing that I am doing something positive. I've seen some inmates begin to turn their lives around. I no longer hate atheists. I no longer hate people. I even like the inmates in the group. I am sensitive to their experiences. I have come to understand them at some level. I'm not in any position to forgive them, nor do I condone their crimes. I'm here to help them in their spiritual journey. Maybe the group meetings will help them to lead more pro-social lives outside the prison walls. Maybe they will never commit a crime again. Maybe!

My sensitivity and religion has opened a door to my purpose in life. I am giving these men what I have always wanted to be given to me: empathic patience and understanding.

I have forgiven Norman for his atheism, as God would have me do so; and I no longer refer to him as AbNorman. I have written to Norman's family and apologized. I have asked for their forgiveness and prayers. I am a changed man; but still a very religious man. I have not found God. I have merely strengthened my belief in Him. Amen!

Addendum

Last week, after the group session, and the inmates were walking out the door, the last inmate stopped and turned to me. He had been silent during the meeting.

"May I say something?" He asked.

"Yes, of course." I replied.

"I don't believe in God. I was not raised that way. I'm not sure if this group is for me."

I walked up to within two feet of him, and I eked out the words "I think I can help you."

******

"Faith is a higher faculty than reason." Philip James Bailey

"*Faith is the antiseptic of the soul."* Walt Whitman

* National Institute of Occupational Safety & Health (NIOSH, 2021)

Introduction

In times of difficulty, many people turn to prayer. Prayer takes many forms. It can be spoken aloud alone or in or with a group of people. It can also be very private. A person can pray silently to oneself; even if only by thoughts, wishes, hopes.

People pray for various reasons...more money, a house, a job, love, an A on a test. Prayer usually involves asking God for something; or even asking a Saint for something. But there are also prayers of thanks, of gratitude. Those are my favorite and preferred prayers.

The following two stories are reflections on life-well-lived over many years. They are also stories of gratitude and thanks. Some regrets are normal; but the joys far outweigh the pains.

The Altar Boy

There is a feeling of Eternity in youth which makes us amends for everything.

To be young is to be as one of the Immortals.

-- *William Hazlitt (1778-1830) Table Talk*

We sometimes have a yen to go back and take a trip down memory lane. In my case, I literally did just that. Instead of Memory Lane, it was Pecan Lane. All the streets in my childhood neighborhood were named after nuts: Pecan, Walnut, Acorn, Almond, Chestnut, Hazelnut, just to name a few. I used to think that the names fit because of all the somewhat nutty people I grew up around.

The church of my childhood is nestled across town in a poor area I had not ventured into for many years. So yesterday after lunch, I set out on this journey back in time and place. The city bus picked me up on schedule. The bus stop is only a block and a half from the church, an easy walk. When I was actually standing in front of that old religious edifice for the first time in over 60 years, it seemed eerie and surreal to me.

I slowly walked up the flight of concrete stairs to the massive front doors. It was quiet, and nobody was around. My shaking of the ornate, brass door lever sounded so loud that I could even hear the echo from the inside. It was locked. I walked around to the side entrance, leading to the Rectory.

The side portal was open, so I went in. It was (is) a beautiful church with marble floors, perfectly maintained but dusty, wooden pews, colorful stained glass windows on two sides, and, front and center, an elaborately decorated altar with Spanish designed gold trimmed spires. Above the center of the altar was the statue of

Jesus, holding the Sacred Heart; to the left was the statue of Virgin Mary and to the right was that of St. Joseph. To the far left of the altar stood the statue of Our Lady of Guadalupe, Matron of the Americas and to the far right was the statue of St. Jude, Patron of Lost Causes. This was the beloved sanctuary of my youth.

The air was stale, with light remnants of a scent of incense. The stillness activated my senses. I could still smell and see the smoke from the incense in the air; and I could hear the organ playing with the two-woman choir singing church songs in Spanish. It was cold inside. The church was not only empty, but it felt like it had been empty for a long time. I sat down comfortably on a squeaky back row pew so that I might reminisce on memories long ago of my time here as an Altar Boy.

Back then, there were two priests: Father Ignacio, then in his late 60s, and Father David, much younger, in his 20s and recently ordained and graduated from the seminary. Father Ignacio was old school, conservative, strict, by the book - the Good Book - and very traditional. Father David was progressive, energetic, liberal, engaging, and very non-traditional. They would occasionally lock horns, but they nevertheless respected each other. They were Yin and Yang, Mutt and Jeff. They were good examples of both harmony and balance for the parishioners to follow. And the members of the congregation respected them without question.

During my time as an acolyte, I can recall several individuals and incidents which stood out for me. For example, one Sunday morning, Father Ignacio was saying Mass, when in the middle of the service, there was a loud yell from the back of the church.

"Lord...Lord God, have mercy on me! Lord God, forgive me....Help me! Please, Lord, give me your mighty blessing. I am a lost man... a sinner!"

It was Sarge. That's what everybody called him. He was a black homeless alcoholic, a veteran of WWII, who would roam the streets of the neighborhood at all hours. He was considered harmless and was generally ignored by everyone. People did feel sorry for him because he seemed so needy and lonely. He refused to live in a shelter when it was offered to him. He always reeked of sweat, alcohol and cigarettes. And, he was often seen talking to himself. "Crazy old Sarge!" He had no known relatives in the area and he seemed to be walking through life isolated and solitary.

His powerful voice shook the parishioners. Father Ignacio was so startled that he jumped when he heard the shout. The women gasped. The men turned as if they had heard a gunshot. I was kneeling at the altar, and stood up in complete surprise and fear. I turned to see Sarge, all six-feet five of him, standing in the middle of the aisle with his hands in the air, as if reaching for God Himself. He was crying, tears washing his face, and he was clearly in a very distressed state.

Several men, including Father David, who was standing in the rear near the confessionals, ran up to Sarge and, as gently as they could, took him by his arms and led him out of the church through the side door. I learned later that he was taken to the hospital where they did a psychiatric evaluation and then kept him on a special ward to treat his condition. He had what was then known as shell-shock or battle fatigue, a nervous condition resulting from his experience during the war. He eventually ended up on a special ward at the VA Hospital. We all felt bad for Sarge, but he really shook us up that morning.

On another occasion, Fr. Ignacio was again saying the Sunday Mass. After the blessings, it was time for the sermon. I took a seat in a corner to hear God's word. Fr. Ignacio mounted the five steps up to the pulpit. He tapped the microphone, and then began what I thought would be his sermon.

"Good people of the Parish: Don't come to me with your bruises and scratches, missing teeth, swollen faces and black eyes. Don't come to me for help. I can't help you. If you are the victim of abuse, don't expect the church to help. Let me tell you this. If someone, anyone, hits you, it's because they don't like you. Regardless of what they tell you, they may not even love you. When someone hits you, and I don't care who it is, call the police. And if you have to, file charges against that person. If the abuse continues, get a lawyer and file for a divorce or for some type of legal separation order. That is how you deal with this problem. That is how you stop the abuse. I can't help you. The church can't help you. I can only pray that you will do the right thing. Get out of that abusive relationship. It's your choice."

He turned and stepped down from the pulpit and continued with the service. The congregation was quiet, but people were turning and looking at each other as if to say "What was that all about?" It later became clear what that was all about. And it had a positive effect on those who heard this message. Domestic abuse and assault had been a covert problem in our community. But after Fr. Ignacio's admonishment, the problem became less frequent, and people began talking more openly about it. And some women made police reports and filed for divorces.

This was a complex message because the Catholic Church had long forbidden divorce. The Old Testament suggests that divorce could be acceptable in some circumstances and with the issuance of a "certificate." The Catholic Church may, in certain circumstances allow a divorce, but only after an official annulment is sanctioned by the diocese. Nevertheless, Father

Ignacio's message seemed to say that abuse was a valid reason for divorce, both legally and morally.

Everyone considered me to be a good altar boy. My mother kept my black cassock and white surplice (sometimes referred to as a cotta) laundered and pressed for every mass that I served. For most of my tenure, I served Monday through Friday at the seven a.m. Mass and also funerals and at special weekend Masses, such as for weddings, confirmations, and baptisms; and at High Masses on Holy Days, namely New Year's Eve at Midnight, Easter, Christmas Eve and Christmas. Of course, there were times when the other servers could not keep their assignments. The priest would call our house, and request that I substitute. And I did. During the 50's and part of the 60's, Masses were in Latin. I had already stopped serving when Spanish and English were incorporated into the ritual.

Despite being a good altar boy, I was somewhat of a curious and mischievous kid. One day after helping Fr. Ignacio to remove his vestments, I stayed to tidy-up the sacristy. He left the sacristy, and, alone, I was free to investigate that hallowed room. I noticed that Fr. Ignacio had forgotten to close the door of the safe all the way. The door was left ajar – an oversight by the old padre. I looked inside. There was no money, but it was where the priests stored the cruets, wine, hosts, extra chalices and other paraphernalia used during Mass. I couldn't resist testing the sweet smelling liquid in a dark quart-sized bottle. It was strange, but tasty, and it burned my mouth and throat. I didn't like it at first. As if to defy the burn in my throat, I took a second sip, and it seemed a bit milder, pleasant, and even stimulating. I then put everything back in its place, closed and locked the safe.

Sometime later, back home, my dad and uncle were out on our patio playing the guitar and accordion, which they often did on weekends. On the table between them was a bottle of alcohol, which they partook of as the evening progressed. I asked my dad if I could have a taste. He hesitated, laughed a little, and then said "Oh, okay. But just a sip." I immediately recognized the taste.

"Dad, that's the same kind of wine the Priests drink at Mass."

"No, *Mijo*. I don't think so. This is not wine. This is bourbon, kinda like whisky."

"But I'm sure it's the same wine Father Ignacio drinks from the chalice. I'm sure of it."

"So, how do you know this? Don't tell me you drank some of the church wine! Did you?"

"No. I didn't drink it; I just sipped it ... once."

My dad and uncle looked at each other and laughed. "Well then, my son, if it's the same thing you tasted, then it's not wine they're drinking. It's whisky."

In a firm voice, he added, "And don't you ever do that again. I forbid it. If I find out you tried that again, I'll tell the priests about it, and you will be punished and not be allowed to serve Mass ever again. You got it?"

That's when I discovered that one or both priests liked whisky. It didn't matter to me whether it was whisky or wine. I thought *maybe when Jesus changed the water to wine, He did so only because maybe whisky had not yet been invented. And is it still the "blood of Christ?"*

I was so good at what I did, I was always asked to help train the new altar boys. The turnover rate was high. The boys would get frustrated or could not keep their scheduled serving times, or they experienced personal issues that inhibited their ability to fulfill their obligations and commitments. The novices were usually undisciplined and seemed to always give me a hard time. They did not like being told what to do by a peer their own age. Most of the boys worked out fine, albeit if only temporarily.

There was one boy I clearly remember. Jordy. He was a quiet kid, shy, and with little eye contact. What stood out for me was that he often appeared to be crying during Mass. His eyes would swell up, and I could see the tears in them. Father David also noticed and one day approached the boy.

"Jordy, is there something wrong? Tell me. Maybe I can help."

There was no response from Jordy.

Father continued "Is it something at school or at home? Would you like me to talk to your parents?"

Jordy's face stiffened "No. It's nothing. I'll be fine... really!"

Jordy always insisted that there was nothing wrong. He would stand his ground and reiterate that he was fine. He denied any problems. I thought it might be allergies. The incense can sometimes do that to people. One day when we were alone I asked.

"Jordy, do you have allergies? Maybe it's the smoke from the incense. Is that why you always look like you're about to cry?"

"No. I don't think I have allergies. I just sometimes feel like crying, and I don't know why."

"Well, there's got to be a reason. People don't just cry for nothing."

He looked down at the marble floor. He did not respond for a long time. But I was feeling patient and waited for a response. When he finally did reply, he had wiped his face and held his chin up, almost in defiance.

"I hate my parents. I hate them so much. I come to Mass, and I'm supposed to be a good altar boy, a good kid; and I'm supposed to forgive and pray for my parents. The Bible says *Honor thy Father and thy Mother*. But I hate them. I don't want to be around them."

Jordy was an only child. His parents were young and poor. But they were very religious, and very strict with him. I was taken aback by what he said.

"Why do you hate your parents? I'm sure they love you. They give you stuff...right?"

Jordy lifted his surplice and unbuttoned his cassock and removed it. He lifted his tee-shirt and exposed his torso. There were bruises, scratches, and other discolorations. He also exposed his back side. There were small but distinct welts. He covered himself up.

"Does it hurt?" I asked.

"Not now. Maybe just a little."

"Why didn't you tell Father David?"

"Because Father Ignacio said not to tell him if things like this happen. I guess the same goes for Father David. The priests and the church can't help. And anyway, they don't care about kids. They don't have any."

I thought that Father Ignacio was talking about adults. But then I realized that the same could be said about kids like Jordy and me.

"Jordy", I said. "If the church or the priests can't help you, somebody should be able to do something. I wish I could do something to help. It just aint right. You need to tell someone who can help you."

"I don't know. I'm scared. You have parents who love you. I don't know what that's like. You don't know how I feel. But, I'll think about it" he mumbled.

Several months later, I learned that Jordy had been taken from his parents and placed in the custody of CFS (Child & Family Services). His parents were accused of child abuse. It really made me sad when I heard that, but at the same time I was relieved, because it was probably the best thing for Jordy.

I think of him even today. He was a good kid, a victim of parents who just didn't know any better or just didn't care. Maybe they didn't love him. Maybe Jordy felt unloved by the very people who were supposed to love him the most. But did he really hate them? Or did he just want to feel loved by them and wanted them to stop hitting him?

I lost contact with Jordy after that. A few years later, my brother told me that he had run into him and that they had an interesting conversation. Jordy had been staying with foster parents who were very kind and loving toward him. He said that Jordy did well in school and athletics. He excelled in track and field in high school and became a long-distance runner. He told my brother that he liked long-distance running because it made him feel independent, free, and safe. Even though he ran alone for up to four hours at a time, it gave him much needed solace. I was very relieved to hear this.

I don't know what happened to Jordy after that. Maybe I'm too nostalgic, but this is difficult for me. I can't accept not knowing what happened later in life to people I knew and cared about. What became of them? What became of Jordy? Is he happy today? Did he eventually outgrow his miserable childhood? I pray that he did. I just can't imagine not having loving parents. I hope Jordy has learned self-love. That would be the first step on his path to recovery. I also believe that he understood his life would always be a long-distance journey.

There was another altar boy who served with me. His name was Erik. Erik was a scrawny runt, but friendly and smart. His favorite expression was "No way." He always said that whenever something surprised him or when he wanted to finalize a topic or issue. He had one brown eye and one hazel eye; a genetic condition called Heterochromia. I remember that he wanted a dog, so his parents searched all the nearby counties for the right dog. They finally found a cute, little terrier which also had this condition. Erik was very happy with his little friend with the different color eyes.

One morning during Mass, without warning, Erik collapsed onto the floor in front of the altar. The congregation gasped. Fr. David turned and then hurried down the steps. He lifted the boy into his arms and carried him over to the Baptismal Font. He cupped some Holy Water into one hand and splashed it on Erik's face several times. Erik eventually regained consciousness. He opened his eyes, somewhat bewildered.

"What happened?" he asked.

"You fainted", Fr. David told him.

"No way!"

It turned out that Erik was anemic or diabetic or something like that, and he had not eaten in over 24 hours. *"No way."* Fr. David later talked to his parents, and it never happened again. After that I became somewhat protective of Erik. I saw myself acting as if I were his big brother. We became good friends. But over the years, we lost contact. I miss Erik.

Fr. David and Fr. Ignacio were so very different that they even said Mass differently. Fr. Ignacio had a deep, slow voice, and people often complained that they could not hear him. On the pulpit, he was loud because of the microphone.

Fr. David never used the pulpit or the microphone. He would give the sermon while standing in the middle of the church aisle and preach as if he were merely talking to the people. He had a great voice that carried to the back of the church. And he would walk up and down the aisle and come close to the parishioners and even touch them on the shoulder. He once told the congregation that Christ did not need a microphone or a pulpit. The voice of Christ preaching on the mountain top could be heard all the way down in the valley. "The Word of God reaches far and wide", he said.

I would say that Fr. David was more popular than Fr. Ignacio. When they heard confessions on Saturdays, the line waiting to confess to Fr. David was much longer than Fr. Ignacio's.

Fr. David was also more attractive, even handsome. Some women of the parish were a little smitten by him. They would always congregate around him and act charming and coy. Dare I say, they even flirted with him! Fr. David welcomed this admiration and took it all in. He seemed to like the attention, innuendos and all.

As mentioned earlier, I was considered an above average altar boy. People would often tell me that I made a really good server to the priests and to the congregation. I was finally and officially recognized near the end of my last month of service when I was given the "Certificate of the Knights of the Altar." In fancy print, it said "This is to certify that Peter Robles is a Full-fledged Member of the Sacred Heart Unit of the Society of the Knights of the Altar;" and then below in smaller letters "and has solemnly pledged to live and die befitting one who has dedicated himself to the service of Our Lord, Jesus Christ."

I was and am very proud of this certificate. I still have it. It sits in the drawer of my night stand, and I sometimes take it out to admire it and remember my life as an acolyte and wine taster. Mostly, it reminds me of how strong my faith and dedication were back then.

Back to yesterday! I sat in that pew for a long time thinking about the altar boys, the priests, and the members of the congregation, and the neighborhood. But then I realized it was getting late, and I needed to catch the 4:00 o'clock bus back. I got up and exited from where I entered. Once outside, the wind blew into my eyes. I rubbed them and refocused.

That is when I saw an older woman walking toward me from the Rectory.

"Can I help you?" she asked.

"Oh, no. Thank you. I was just stopping by to visit the church. I was an altar boy here many years ago."

She stared into my now blood-shot eyes as if reading them.

"I know who you are. You're, or you were, that Robles boy. You don't remember me? Angie?"

I examined her face, and it came back to me. *Yes, she's Angie*, the young girl/woman who took care of the Rectory. Angie came to live in the Rectory after she was orphaned around age 16. She was the housekeeper, cook, laundress, and all-around caretaker of the Rectory and the Priests. She was always quiet and unassuming. Not many people even noticed her, except when they needed to contact the priests. Angie would screen them first or answer all their questions and concerns so as not to trouble the Fathers. Angie was about six or seven years older than me, and she was pretty back then, still is. I guess I had always had a boyish crush on her.

"Yes, of course I know who you are. I just didn't recognize you at first. It's been so long, you know. So you still live here in the Rectory, even though the church basically no longer has services and is non-functional?"

"Well, people still come by...like you. So the diocese said that I could stay and look after the place...you know...maintain it. I'm kinda like a caretaker. They pay all the bills and give me a small monthly stipend. And I get to live here for free."

"That's great, Angie. So, what happened with the priests?"

"Well, as you might have guessed, Fr. Ignacio passed many years ago. And Father David...well, I married him."

Shocked and even a little stunned, I said "No Way!"

"We fell in love. David approached the diocese and told them he wanted to leave the priesthood, which was not allowed, as you know. But somehow, he negotiated with the Bishop, and he was ordained the Deaconship here. Deacons can marry. A few months later, we had the wedding here in the church. It was wonderful. Praise God! It was the happiest time in my life."

"Wow. Congratulations. And, so, where is Father David...I mean David?"

"Oh, he passed on two years ago. He had a heart condition. So it's just me living here alone. We did not have any children. I could not have a child due to an early hysterectomy. But we were very happy while we were married. And church responsibilities kept us both very busy."

I was blown away, but kept my composure. I felt a warmth while talking to Angie. This may sound crazy, but I felt the presence of Fr. David. He was looking down on us...smiling. Meeting up with Angie also rekindled the attraction I had for her back when I was an altar boy.

Angie went on talking about other matters of the past and of the church we so loved. But again, I was aware of the time passing quickly.

"Angie, I've got to get going or I'll miss my bus. I'll call you sometime."

"But we hardly talked about you, Peter. Do you still live in town? What about your family?"

"We'll talk more about me later. I promise. Just give me your number, and I'll get back in touch with you soon."

She gave me the number, and I hurried off to the bus stop. I made it on time, just as the bus was approaching. I got on the bus and sat in the rear seat. There were only a few passengers.

I figured I'd be back at the home in about 30 minutes. I thought *They are probably frantically looking for me. Maybe thinking something bad may have happened to me. They might have already notified the police – missing person - and next of kin. I bet they searched every room in that nursing home. I bet they panicked when they couldn't find me. I didn't tell anyone I was leaving. I just snuck out unnoticed. I'm still a little mischievous.*

When I saw the old pink and green sign "GENTLE ARMS – A Retirement Community Residence", I suspected I'd have some explaining to do. I knew the staff would be relieved to see me, but also somewhat upset with me. That's okay! I got back here just in time for dinner. We eat around five, five-thirty.

I had a great day-trip yesterday. And I, unexpectedly, got to see Angie. What a pleasant surprise that was!

The staff at the nursing home was indeed upset with me. They did not call the authorities, but they did call hospitals and a family member (on file as the contact person). They also checked with businesses nearby. One of the residents told staff that I was hiding in one of the unused rooms. There were also rumors that I was kidnapped. Much ado about nothing! I was castigated for leaving without notifying anyone. One of the nurses even said "bad boy", as if I were a dog or a pet.

"Where have you been? Where did you go?" they asked.

Feeling just a little imposed on, I mumbled "Downtown and around. On the bus."

I thought, *Should I tell the staff where I went? Should I tell them about Angie? Should I tell them that I plan to go see her again ... soon?*

Ni modo ... No way!

Introduction

Dreamers and believers; Theologians and Philosophers. They will tell you their concept of what awaits us after death. But they don't know any more than the guy or gal at the checkout counter. We know absolutely nothing about what happens after we die. We like to believe in something that comforts us. We all talk to dead people.

Is there "something" after death; or is there "nothing" after death. And why does it matter? I believe what matters is what we know and feel about our lives, how we have lived. That is what matters.

In this last story, Paloma reflects on her life. She evaluates her life-long decisions in the face of obstacles and confrontations. She recognizes what has given her joy and what has given her pain. And more importantly, how she responded to it all. That is what really matters.

The Love Seat

Better by far you should forget and smile,
Than that you should remember and be sad.
--Christina Rossetti (1830-1894) A Birthday

Paloma, approaching octogenarian status at 79, was living alone in a small house on 10th Avenue. She was a widow, her husband having died from a rare heart disease when he was only 59. That was over 20 years ago. And she, being the strong independent woman that she was, chose to live alone and handle her own affairs.

But time and bad health began to take over her life, and despite her objections, with her daughter's encouragement, she decided it best that she move into an assisted living environment. In her younger years, she would say "You'll never catch me in one of those places. People just go there to die." Now, she was mentally ready to accept the change. Like death, change is inevitable, and Paloma recognized that truth, that reality. Tomorrow, with the help of her daughter, she would make the move to her new home.

She was finishing the day packing up the last few things she wanted to take with her to the small, but nicely furnished, apartment. She stood in the doorway of the large den, which for many years had served as the gathering place for friends and family to share each others' company. The room had looked the same for decades, cluttered with a mixture of old furniture and antiques. Most of the pieces were inherited from her grandmother and mother.

Ah, she thought. *Such memories*!

She turned to leave toward her bedroom when she unexpectedly heard a voice.

"Don't send me to the Goodwill. Take me with you."

She was taken aback, startled. She turned around to look back into the den. No one was there. She scanned from wall to wall. Nothing! *I must be going crazy* she thought. *I swear I heard someone say something. Maybe I'm hallucinating in my old age.* She again faced in the direction of her bedroom, still a little shaken by the experience.

"You're not hallucinating, my dear Paloma."

She was unnerved by the sound of the voice. The speaker even knew her name. Shocked, she looked directly at the love seat near the bay window, where the voice came from.

"Yes, it is I, who speak to you, sweet Paloma. Your life-long comforter! We've been together for so many years. You can't just move away and leave me here. I'll end up in a strange place like you. We need each other – you and me. After all, we've been through a lot!"

Paloma was in disbelief. Surely she had lost her mind, her sense of reality. *Maybe,* she thought, *someone is playing a trick on me.*

"Who's there?" she demanded aloud.

"Just me" the love seat responded.

Paloma was frightened and confused. Incredulous!

"Okay. This is crazy. You're a chair, a couch, a sofa for crying out loud!"

"Wrong on two of the nomenclatures! I'm a love seat, a sofa for two. That's important because you are one person, no longer a part of a couple or a pair...just a separate One."

Paloma rubbed her temples, then her eyes, then shook her head in the negative. "No, I'm not crazy, and I'm not talking to a piece of furniture. This is nuts!"

"I resent being called a piece of furniture. I'm a comforter. I have comforted and counseled family and friends for many years, especially you. Now, I want you to listen to me."

Paloma stood vexed and bewildered. And yet, she gave in to her primal instincts.

"Okay, love seat, go ahead! I'm listening. But this is madness. I've got to wake up from this. Maybe I need a drink."

"You don't drink. Alcohol is not your friend. You know this from past experiences. Let me begin with your beautiful grandmother, or grandmamma, as you called her. She loved you more than you will ever know. When you were an infant, she sat here many an evening with you in her arms. She would hold you tightly, rock you, and kiss you all over and tell you how special you were. You would cry and she would comfort you and eventually make you feel better, and you would stop crying, and fall into your baby-world sleep. This was her favorite place to bring you. I comforted both of you. Even during nursery and first grade, you would come here to sit on her lap. She gave you the hugs you couldn't get from your mother...or your father. Your parents were not lovable or loving; so you tried to love them, but you were afraid of them. You eventually realized that if you truly love someone, you never fear them."

"Why are you telling me these things? And who are you?" Paloma was almost in tears. After all these years, she still missed her grandmamma and feared the memory of her parents.

"Because you want to abandon me -- just as you were emotionally abandoned by your parents. I want you to understand that when your grandmother married your grandfather, she did not love him. She loved the idea of getting married. And after your grandfather died, you may recall that she sat here and shared this truth with you. She went on to tell you that over the years of their marriage, she had learned to love him more than anyone in her whole life. She had told him 'you are my life...please don't leave me'. He died knowing that your grandmother loved him totally. Yet, she felt abandoned when he passed on. You have inherited that sense of abandonment. So have I. Please don't leave me. We need each other."

"How do you know all these things? That was many years ago. You're scaring me. I need to know what's happening here. Who are you?"

"You never even considered abandoning me -- until now.

"After your grandmother died, your parents became more present in your life, and not in a good way. They fought a lot. All the arguing and yelling eventually turned to aggression and violence. You see this dark stain on my right arm? It's a blood stain. It's where your mother laid her head after your father hit her in the face. Blood from her nose and mouth soaked into my worn upholstery. She tried to clean out the stain, but the blotch is still noticeable. It's a scar on my arm. It's a bruise that will not go away. You sat next to her here and tried to comfort her.

"This was not the first time, and it would not be the last. You felt helpless and useless. And your mother told you to mind your own business; that this was between her and your father. That made you very sad. You never understood why this happened, except that it had something to do with your father's drinking. Also, you suspected that he had 'girlfriends'.

"Eventually, your mother had had enough. After nearly 20 years, she filed for a divorce. This was very hard for her. She was not a happy person before the divorce, and afterwards, she became even less responsive to you and everyone else. She retreated into herself. She would sit here and self-medicate with a variety of pills. You wanted her to stop and told her so. She snapped at you, and ordered you to stay out of her affairs.

"It was around that time that you met Diego. He was so cute, charming, and a real talker. He liked you. You felt loved, wanted, cared for. Suddenly <u>you</u> mattered to someone."

"Stop!"Paloma interrupted. "Don't say any more. Don't go there! That's personal."

"It's all personal, Paloma. You and Diego couldn't control yourselves; and like so many horny teens, you two ended up having sex – not thinking about the consequences. And yes, it was no surprise that nearly three months later you realized that you were pregnant. You were devastated. You liked Diego, but you could not see yourself spending the rest of your life with him. You sat here and cried your eyes out for several days. I tried to comfort you. I told you that you could not have this baby. I warned you of the consequences. You and I considered all the possible outcomes of having a child, as well as how your life would change if you had the baby. I know how difficult it was for you because you felt that there was no one to turn to. You felt very much alone in that predicament. And you were!

"Eventually, you decided that you should not have this baby. This was the hardest decision of your life. We concluded that how others judged you did not matter. You are not a religious person, but you felt that only God had the right to judge your decision and actions. Let God be the judge of you, if that is His purview. That is how you, and I, saw it.

"Then we devised a plan, a dumb but effective plan. You told Diego about your pregnancy. He agreed to give you money to help abort the baby and pay for your out-of-town stay for a month. You both swore to keep this between you. On the designated day, you packed some things and 'ran away', not telling your mother. The town you went to was in a bordering state. You were scared. You were barely 16 and alone in a strange town.

You had learned about this doctor and the clinic from the older girls at school. You lied about your age, and no one at the clinic vetted you because you looked older than your age. It almost seemed too easy.

"The whole procedure took just a short time. Afterward, you returned to the small hotel room you had rented near the clinic. You longed to be sitting here with me. You did not miss your mother, father or Diego. Yet, you had the sensibility to call your mother and tell her you were okay; not to worry; you would be home soon. Your mother seemed unconcerned, detached. You vowed never to tell anyone, except Diego, about the abortion. This was between you and God and me."

Paloma wiped the tears with her smock. "Okay, you win. I'm a bad, terrible, cold person."

"No, my dear. You are a survivor. You gave it your best shot and did what you had to do. It took a lot of courage, not to mention risk. You did regret it for a long time, but, again, time brings about its own changes. Anybody who tells you that they have no regrets is fooling themselves. You're not like that. You accepted what you did, and you carried on; forward, not backward. You realized that when someone has a regret, it means they've learned something.

"You returned home to a cold mother and a house with no spirit. She never even asked you why you ran away or where you went. She was only concerned about herself. You only found solace in the comfort I provided for you. Many a night, you would curl up in a fetal position and cry yourself to sleep right here. Things were so bad at home, you almost regretted returning. You knew that you had to get away from this toxic environment. The only way to do that was to get married. A husband would at least take you away from this miserable existence.

"You decided that you would find a man to marry, even if you did not love him. After all, you recalled that your grandmother did not love your grandfather when they married. Maybe you too could learn to love your husband, once you were married and had lived together for a while."

"And I did. I cared for him so much. Things worked out just fine." Paloma said excitedly.

"Yes, you did learn to love and appreciate Larry. He turned out to be kind, considerate, responsible, family man. He worked hard and provided for you and your two children. He loved you very much. After he died, you said that you had a 'half-life', that you were not complete. Larry made you feel complete. Eventually, you learned that you did not need a man, or anyone else for that matter, to be complete. That's when you became your own woman.

"And your daughter -- because of you, she is a beautiful and wonderful person; and so are your loving grandchildren and great-grandchildren."

"And my devoted 'altar boy' son? What happened? Where did I go wrong with him?"

"You are not responsible for your son. As an altar boy he learned all that was good. Outside the church walls, he learned much that was bad. He chose the wrong path at the fork in the road. He had a lot of both your father and your mother in him. His imprisonment was inevitable. Many a night, you sat here and tried to talk some sense into him. He would not listen. You lie here and out of anger and frustration, and yes love, you pounded your fists into my left arm until you exhausted yourself. It still saddens you that he will probably die in prison for what he did.

"You still miss him. You forgave him as you did your mother and father. It was difficult and it took many years, but you did. That became your motto over the years: give and forgive. By giving and forgiving you attained some level of peace."

At that moment, Paloma's cell phone rang. She swiped the tears from her cheeks.

"Mom?"

"Yes, Liz. It's me."

"What are you up to, mom?"

"Oh, nothing. Just packing up the last of the things I'm going to take with me tomorrow."

"Good. I was just calling to remind you that Fred and I will be there around eight in the morning to pick you up. They are expecting us at Peaceful Waters about nine."

"Oh, okay. I'll be ready." She paused. "Liz ..."

"Yeah, mom?"

"I've been thinking. I'd like to take that old love seat with me to the new apartment."

"What? Why? Mom, you know that the apartment is already fully furnished."

"I know, dear. But that old love seat has been with me for eons and we've kept it even after all these years. It belonged to your great-grandmamma. I've grown attached to it."

"Mom, I understand. Really I do. But you are going to start with a clean slate. It's time to turn the page. No, I mean close the book on the past. I know all about your childhood in a, quote, 'dysfunctional' family. Grandpa was abusive to you and to grandma. Their divorce didn't make things any better. You were so unhappy ... until you married dad. Up to the day he died, you and dad were the consummate lovebirds. I know you miss him terribly. That's why it's so important for you to put everything about the past behind you and move on. You know I'm right about this. I'm only thinking about your welfare. You know that."

Paloma stared lovingly at the love seat. It was old, discolored, with worn out arms and lumpy cushions.

It's original color unrecognizable, its shape now askew. It even smelled of blood, sweat, and of course, the tears. *Kinda like me* she thought.

"You're right, honey. I'll leave it. It can go with the rest of the stuff to Goodwill or the Salvation Army Store or wherever, after you guys keep what you want. I'll be fine."

"Great, mom! See you in the morning."

Paloma disconnected and put the phone in the pocket of her smock. She did not mention to Liz her conversation with the love seat. Liz would want to take her to see a shrink!

"You know ..." said the love seat, "a brand new 20 dollar bill has the same value as a 20 dollar bill that is old and wrinkled and scuffed, dirtied, and downright ugly. I still value you; maybe more now than ever before. Come sit. Let me give you the comfort you deserve. I'm going to miss you when you're gone. We go back a long way. That means a lot to both of us."

Paloma slowly walked up to the love seat and gently sat down on it. Once again, she felt comfortable and comforted, loved. She wanted to enjoy this moment for the last time.

"Again, I have to ask you: Who are you?"

"You are not alone, Paloma, my dear. I am always with you. I have always been with you. You could say that I've always had your back, your biggest supporter. I'm on your side. I am You."

Paloma settled down on the love seat. She lay on her side, and curled up into a fetal position. She smelled the years of change on the worn out cloth and felt the joys, pains, sorrows -- the gamut of human emotions. She reluctantly understood *now I must let everything go*.

"That's right" the love seat said. "Rest now! Relax! We are going home.

You can let your lungs relax now."

And Paloma allowed herself to take her last breath.

"And, you can let your heart stop now."

And Paloma allowed her heart to stop beating.

*****

And, the next morning, that is just the way her daughter Liz found her: curled up in a fetal position on the love seat; motionless.

As she approached Paloma, her daughter assumed she was peacefully sleeping.

"Mom. Mom, wake up. We're here, Mom ... Mom?"

As Liz got up closer to the love seat and looked down at her mother's face, she noticed that in her slumber, Paloma's eyes were half closed...

Or were they only half open?

About the Author

I have never thought of myself as a writer. I like telling stories. Some of my stories are pretty good, and some are really bad. Nevertheless, I find that most people like my stories.

I grew up in Kansas City, Missouri, but have lived in Texas most of my adult life. I did not move to Texas by choice. Circumstance, and maybe fate, brought me to San Antonio. My experiences here have been both satisfying and inspiring ... and fulfilling.

I have a Bachelor's degree from UMKC, a Master's degree from UTSA, and a Ph.D. from University of Texas, Austin. I was a licensed psychologist for most of my professional life. My practice took me to a prison, a state hospital, nursing homes, as well as college teaching. These stories were written years ago. After retirement, I decided to organize my stories into print. Most of these stories go back to my developmental years and onward. I was an Altar Boy for several years and that experience stayed with me like a tattoo etched on my chest. I hope you like my coming-of-age stories. Please review them. And, I hope you will recommend them to others.

Thanks again! And remember: Stay safe and strong. My best wishes for you! God Bless!

One Final Word

I hope you liked my stories; and I thank you for reading them. Feel free to provide feedback:
danielmacias.phd@gmail.com

Get a copy of Altar Boys Anonymous, a short story collection, for you or someone you know at the following link and tell your friends.

https://Altarboysanonymous.billspositivebooks.com

Thanks again! And remember: It's not growing old that takes the joy out of our lives. It's taking the joy out of our lives that makes us grow old.

www.ingramcontent.com/pod-product-compliance
Lightning Source LLC
Chambersburg PA
CBHW070458200726
48293CB00007B/2281

* 9 7 8 1 9 5 1 7 7 6 9 1 6 *